Take a Bow

Take a Bow

ELIZABETH EULBERG

Point

ISBN 978-0-545-43982-4

10 9 8 7 6 5 4 3 2 1   12 13 14 15 16 17/0

Printed in the U.S.A. 40

This edition first printing, January 2012

The text was set in Palatino.

Book design by Elizabeth B. Parisi

For the biggest rock star in my eyes

DAVID LEVITHAN

editor extraordinaire,
unparalleled karaoke partner,
and above all, my dear friend

"Are teenage dreams so hard to beat?"

— THE UNDERTONES, "Teenage Kicks"

The Auditions

CARTER

*M*y life has been one big audition.

I can't even remember the first audition my mom dragged me to. It was for a diaper commercial back when we were living in LA. I was six months old. While most kids' first memories are of playing with friends, mine are of sitting in cold reception areas waiting for my name to be called. The only plus side was that after I auditioned, Mom rewarded me with McDonald's. That was the only time I ever truly felt like a normal kid.

After I got cast in the first *Kavalier Kids* movie, I didn't have to go on that many auditions. The roles came to me. By the time I was nine, I was on the cover of *People* magazine and a presenter at the Oscars, the basic go-to kid for cute. I was the on-screen "son" of every big-name actor. I've worked with the best. And with the *Kavalier Kids* franchise, I was featured on countless lunch boxes, pillowcases, Happy Meals — you name it, my face was on it. (I don't think I've recovered yet from seeing my toothy grin on a roll of toilet paper. Really, toilet paper. Apparently the studio's marketing division had no shame.)

I'd shoot a big-time movie during the spring and a *Kavalier Kids* movie in the fall (for a major summer release). And even though my childhood was anything but normal, I look back fondly on the *Kavalier Kids* movies. The other child actors were like friends to me. At least they seemed like my friends, or what friends should be. But we only hung out on the set. There were no sleepovers or pizza parties, just on-set tutors and line readings.

Things were great, but then there was a — let's call it an *altercation* between my mom and the producer. I got kicked off the franchise. A new wave of cute kids came into Hollywood and I was relegated to being a featured guest star on network crime shows.

So I made a decision. It was the one thing that scared Mom more than anything, even more than crow's-feet and taxicabs. And it wasn't moving to New York City or starring in a soap opera that was "beneath" me. No, we did those things so I could do the thing that was even scarier to Mom:

High school.

Yes, Carter Harrison, former child megastar and current soap opera actor, wants to go to school.

But as I sit in the hallway at the New York City High School of the Creative and Performing Arts, I know that this isn't a normal school. It's one of the most prestigious performing arts high schools in the country. I knew I could convince my mom to let me go if I talked about how this would help me with my craft.

Yes, I actually used the word *craft* to describe what I do. But my "craft" is more on a par with the caricature artists in Times Square than with a true artist.

I play pretend. I've been doing it my entire life. I've been doing it so long, I don't even know who I am anymore. I'm more comfortable being someone else than being me. I don't even feel like me when I'm "Carter Harrison." The paparazzi were waiting outside the school today when I arrived, and I flashed that famous grin at them . . . but that wasn't me. That was a role.

As we wait for my name to be called, I glance at Mom hiding behind her oversize sunglasses. She didn't seem all that surprised to see the photographers outside. Gee, I wonder who leaked that my audition is today? It's not like being on a soap opera gets you a ton of press, but when you were the biggest box office draw at the age of ten, people like to follow you around. See what you're up to. It's like my life is a never-ending episode of *Where Is He Now?*

At least I've gotten used to the attention. I'm really good at blocking it out. Plus, it helped me get a role on a show that only requires me to work a few hours a week. This way, I stay on television to appease my mom and I get to go to school for me.

I'm not even nervous as I wait for my name to be called. Stepping onto that stage and reciting my two monologues (one from *Our Town* and the other from *You're a Good Man, Charlie Brown*) will be easy. That's a normal day for me. But the thought of getting to go to school is what will make me nervous.

What's ironic is that Mom is the one who doesn't want me to go to school. She thinks I won't be prepared to handle being in a school with other kids.

Let's see, I've spent my entire life being judged, critiqued, and picked apart.

I think I'm more ready for high school than anybody could be.

SOPHIE

*I*t's all going according to plan.

This audition is just one more box to check off on Sophie's Plan to Superstardom.

Basically, the list so far has consisted of me performing at every possible talent show, wedding, sporting event, bar mitzvah, birthday party, etc., in the Brooklyn area (check!), getting Emme to write me a can't-lose original song for my audition (check!), and getting into CPA.

Of course, once I'm accepted, I'll have my work cut out for me. I'm not that naïve. So once I get in I need to become the star pupil, land the lead in every play, get the most coveted spot in the Senior Showcase, and then get a record contract by the time I graduate.

I will have a Grammy before I turn twenty. Even if it kills me.

I'm not even nervous. Are you kidding me? I LOVE being onstage. I LOVE the glow of the spotlight. It's the waiting that's killing me.

I look around and notice a few other contenders for the vocal department at CPA from different talent contests that I've done . . . and won. They've got nothing on me and they know it.

All the singers (at least in Brooklyn) are jealous of me. While they'll be auditioning with songs from *West Side Story*, *My Fair Lady*, and *The Sound of Music*, I have an original Emme Connelly song written just for me.

For a second, just a second, my stomach drops. I hope Emme gets in. Her audition for the music composition program is in a couple weeks. Although her acceptance (or rejection) won't really affect my Plan. She'll still write songs for me. It would just be easier if she would also be at my school. Don't get me wrong, she's talented enough to get in, but being center stage really isn't her thing. She gets nervous.

Not everybody can be a natural.

"Sophie Jenkins."

I hear my name and enter the auditorium. I can't wait to show the panel what I'm capable of. I'm ready to move on with my Plan and be the star that I know I am.

This is just one small step.

Check.

ETHAN

I want to get this over with.

My stomach has been in knots all morning. Oh, who am I kidding? I've been a wreck since I got the date of this audition. Maybe going to CPA isn't the best idea. I've got it pretty good in Greenwich. I've got friends, and even better, I've got Kelsey.

Although, I just got a girlfriend and what do I do? I audition for a school in New York City, which means I'll have to live at my parents' Park Avenue apartment during the week.

Leave it to me to complicate one of the few good things in my life.

I almost considered backing out of the audition and not going to CPA, but — and I'm fully aware of how corny this sounds — music is my life.

At first I didn't know that it was unusual for someone to hear a song and be able to play it back instantly on the piano or guitar. Or that not everybody can sit down and write a song. I've been playing music, *my* music, for as long as I can remember. It flows from me with ease.

It's just the lyrics that I suck at.

I'm a thirteen-year-old kid who lives in a huge house in Connecticut with my investment banker father and stay-at-home mom. What do I have to write about? I don't know anything about suffering or pain. Or love.

I guess the one good thing going for me is that I don't have to sing today. I'm doing a couple of instrumental pieces. I hate singing. I hate it when people look at me. I wonder if they'll let me perform behind a screen?

I try to get my legs to stop shaking, but if they stay still, what will distract me from the bile that is slowly rising in my throat? I go to bite my nails, but there isn't any nail left.

Dad squeezes my shoulder. I hate him knowing that I'm nervous. Why can't I just tune out the voices in my head telling me I'm going to mess it up, like I mess everything up? Why can't I be normal? Why can't I do something without thinking of the fourteen thousand ways that I can mess up?

Actually, there is one thing I can do to quiet the voices. The only thing that I am good at, which is playing music. *That* I can do well.

It's everything else that's the problem.

EMME

$\mathcal{I}$ thought things would be easier the second time around.

But nothing seems to be going according to Sophie's Plan. And it's all my fault.

I don't think there was ever a doubt that Sophie would get into the vocal music program. How could she not? She's amazing. She got her acceptance letter right away ... on the same day that I got my letter telling me that the admissions department was undecided on my application and I had to audition again.

While the CPA letter explained that the reasoning was that they had an "overwhelming" number of applicants for the music composition program's inaugural year, I knew the truth: I wasn't good enough.

I try to hold back the tears that are creeping up. What would the admissions team think if I walked onto the stage in tears? Probably not the best idea.

But I've wanted to go to CPA since I was little. I've wanted this for so long.

And I don't want to disappoint Sophie.

Going to CPA together has been our goal since we first met, when we were eight and both performing at a youth talent show in Prospect Park. I played an original song I wrote on the piano. Sophie sang "Over the Rainbow." But Sophie doesn't just sing, she Sings with a capital *S*. She opens her mouth and time stops. I haven't met a single person who hasn't been mesmerized by her voice and her stage presence.

She even had it back when we were eight. I'll never forget her coming up to me afterward with her gold medal around her neck (I got the silver). She didn't even introduce herself — she didn't need to; everyone there knew who she was. She simply said, "Hi, I like your song. You should write one with words and I'll sing it for you." We've been a team ever since.

It's Sophie who's been my biggest cheerleader from the very beginning. She was the one who planted the seed years ago about going to CPA. We'd be an unstoppable force, a dynamic duo, the greatest singer-and-songwriter team that CPA has ever seen.

But thanks to me, our team is in serious jeopardy.

"Emme Connelly."

My name is called and I try to steady myself as I walk onto the stage.

I try to block out all the doubting thoughts in my head.

I can do it.

I can do it.

I can do it.

This isn't just about me. It's about Sophie.

And if I'm not sure I can do it for me, I know I can do it for her.

Senior Year

EMME

I never in a million years thought I'd be sitting here. Well, truth be told, I think that every time I'm in CPA's auditorium. Freshman year, sitting with Sophie by my side, I couldn't believe I'd made it in. Then sophomore year, I was shocked that I'd survived the first year. Junior year was the biggest surprise since I'd almost wanted to sabotage my audition for that semester because I was so tired — tired of the auditions we have to do to be accepted *each semester*, tired of the extra classes and studios, tired of the concerts, the pressure, the competition. The constant competition.

Fortunately for me, the music composition department is the least competitive of all the programs. Ethan, Ben, Jack, and I work together on pretty much every project, and have since the very first day of school.

But other groups don't have it so easy. Jack's girlfriend, Chloe, is in the dance department, and she has to eat her protein bars in secret during lunch. It's a double competition, to see who can dance the best and eat the least. It's as if being the skinniest person in the group is a badge of honor, not an eating disorder.

The drama department is full of . . . well, drama. I stay far away from anybody in that department when a show is being cast. It's not pretty. Leading up to the auditions, there is backstabbing and sabotage of *Hamlet* proportions, and when the cast list is posted, those without parts are *les misérables*.

And then there's Sophie. As we wait for our first assembly of senior year to begin, I look four rows in front of me to where Sophie is sitting with Carter. Sophie's had it a lot rougher than me and I feel so guilty. After all, if it wasn't for Sophie, I wouldn't even be here.

Ethan taps my knee and motions up front. Dr. Pafford, our principal, strides onto the stage.

"Hello, seniors." He leans on the podium and takes stock of the room. Judging. We are always being judged. "Over ten thousand people applied your freshman year, 624 got in, and today there are only 513 left. Of that you should be proud."

He pauses dramatically. We all know he never gives us a compliment without showing us its downside.

"But now is when we really figure out who will one day appear on this screen." He gestures to the large screen that is rolling down behind him. Our first day of freshman year, we were welcomed with images of CPA alumni: Oscar, Grammy, and Tony winners flashed before our eyes. "As you all know, you are here two weeks before the start of class to discuss the opening-day performances for the freshmen as well as, of course, the Senior Showcase."

It's as if the air has been sucked out of the room at the mention of the showcase. Every January, CPA hosts talent scouts, agents, and college administrators to an evening that highlights the talent at the school. It's the biggest audition of them all. Juilliard, Alvin Ailey, William Morris — they all come.

The mere thought of it makes me sick.

Both Ethan and Ben nudge me. They know me so well.

Dr. Pafford continues, "We will be holding auditions for the spots in the freshman welcome program next week. You'll have three minutes. We have only ten performance spots available. Sign-up sheets will be up next Monday. And remember, everything you do this semester, and I do mean *everything*, will weigh in on who will be invited to perform in the showcase."

He dismisses us, and groups immediately start to form.

"So, lunch?" Jack says as he stretches and pats his stomach. "I'm going to need a full stomach before I can even think of what torture you two will make me endure for this gig." He nods at Ethan and me.

"Sure, um . . ." I say, then stop. We all see Sophie approach me, a smile on her face. I smile back. I haven't seen her that much over the summer and we haven't been able to get together since she got back from her family vacation. This is the longest we've been apart since we were eight, and I've really missed her.

"Hey, Em!" Sophie hugs me. "I've missed you!"

I hug her back. "Me, too! I can't wait to show you what I've been working on."

Sophie claps her hands enthusiastically. "You know I'm dying to hear it."

She turns to the guys and gives them all a little wave.

"Hey, Sophie, nice to see you show up, just in time to get a song from Emme," Jack says drily. "How convenient."

We both ignore him.

"The guys and I are heading to lunch," I say. "How about tonight?"

She looks disappointed. "I'd love to meet tonight, but Carter has this thing, some opening of something, and I promised him I'd go along." I love how Sophie makes it sound like work. I know that she loves going to openings with Carter: the photographers, the attention, the coverage. We are complete opposites when it comes to that.

We settle on tomorrow afternoon after she consults her schedule and Carter's. There's always been some tension between Sophie and the guys, but they don't get it. They just see Sophie singing my songs, but they have no idea (no matter how many times I've tried to explain it) how much I rely on her.

She gives my songs a voice.

When it comes down to it, I need her a whole lot more than she needs me.

★　★　★　★　★　★　★　★　★　★　★　★　★　★

"So!" Jack gives us a smile after we order our food at the diner. This can only mean trouble. "This feels like the first day of school and we're eating lunch. . . ."

Ethan and Ben groan. I try to contain a smile, but it's too hard. It's a tradition. It started back on our first day of school, when we all met.

That first day, I walked into the cafeteria like a prisoner being sent to death row. I'd been dreading going to the cafeteria by myself since Sophie and I realized we had different lunch periods. To make matters worse, I hadn't made a single friend all morning.

The cafeteria was filled with students already settled into their groups, laughing and enjoying themselves.

I looked over and saw a boy from music composition eating a sandwich by himself. I didn't know his name, but Mr. North had said he was the only person who didn't have to re-audition to get in. I headed over to him, knowing that I needed to make an effort to get to know people.

"Hey, I'm Emme," I said. He looked up at me, mid-bite. His black hair was cut extremely short, almost a buzz cut, and it couldn't hide his ruddy cheeks. Also, he was wearing a T-shirt and jeans that were both about four sizes too big. "Um, we're in music composition together?" I didn't know why I'd made that sound like a question. "Um, can I join you?" My voice went up an octave higher than normal.

He nodded. Then, after he finished swallowing his food, he finally spoke. "I'm Ethan."

"Hi." I opened up my lunch sack and pulled out a bag of carrots. "Um, so . . ." I couldn't think of anything to say. I wanted to ask about his audition, the kind of songs he wrote, what he played, pretty much everything about him. "I can't believe I'm here, you know? My friend Sophie, she's in the vocal program and she's so good. She has a different lunch period. I was so worried about finding someone to sit with at lunch and I'm so excited to see you."

I remember thinking: *You know, Emme, there is a reason why you let Sophie do all the talking.*

Ethan smiled politely at me.

"Hey!" a new voice called out. I ignored it. "Hey, Red!" I looked up to see two guys from class standing over us. "Got room at your table for two more?"

"Of course!" I said, grateful to be saved from further embarrassing myself in front of Ethan.

"I'm Jack, this is Ben." Jack had a friendly smile on his face, a bigger build that suited him well, and a massive array of curls on his head.

Ben sat down across from him. That day, he had on a funky green and navy plaid newsboy cap that almost covered his dirty-blond hair. He was *way* more stylish than anybody I'd ever gone to school with.

Jack laughed. "So are you going to tell us your name, or are we going to stick with my nickname for you?"

"My nickname?"

"Yeah, Red. It suits you." He pulled on a strand of my hair.

"Oh!" I tried to laugh it off, but my bright red hair has always made me so self-conscious. As Sophie likes to remind me, often, you can't miss me in a room. "I'm Emme and this is Ethan."

"Ethan!" Jack started nodding his head. "Ethan the chosen one. So did you want to kill North for calling you out in class?"

Ethan shrugged his shoulders.

Jack continued. "'Cause I wouldn't have wanted the attention, I'll tell you that much. From what I can tell, competition here is pretty fierce."

"Please." Ben sighed. "We are in music, so we need other people. No need to get the claws out . . . yet. Plus, I hear first year you get paired off for a bunch of assignments." Ben slammed his hand on the table. "That's it! Right here. We should form a band!"

"I like where this is going." Jack rubbed his hands together. "This is more like it. A brotherhood — no offense." He winked at me. "Red here will be the hot-chick lead singer."

"Oh, I don't sing. But my friend Sophie —" I said it so quietly that Jack moved right on to the next band member.

"What do you play, Ethan?"

Ethan hesitated. "Guitar, piano, sax, drums . . ."

"Okay, we get it. Genius. Emme, how about you?"

"Oh, I play piano and guitar mostly. I played flute when I was little, but . . ."

"Yeah, we don't need a flutist for our awesome rock band."

Ben interrupted. "Why do you automatically assume we're a rock band?"

"Oh, is this our first fight as a band? And things were going so well!" Jack's large belly laugh echoed through the cafeteria. "I can already see the documentary on us now: 'When CPA Cliché started off —' "

"What's *CPA Cliché*?" Ben asked.

"Our band name. What's the most cliché thing to do at CPA? I'll answer that for you: Form a rock band! And we're doing it on the first day. I wonder if we can get extra credit?"

"We are *not* naming our band CPA Cliché," Ben protested.

"So you agree we're in a band, then?" Jack looked around the table. Ethan shrugged and looked at me. All I could think to do was shrug back. I was just happy to have people talking to me.

Ben took a notebook from his bag. "All right, someone needs to be serious about this. Ethan, guitar. Ben, bass. Emme, keyboard-slash-guitar. Jack, drums."

"Oh, so you assume I play drums because I'm a brother?" Jack asks.

"No, I assume you play drums because you've been knocking out a beat with your silverware since we sat down." Ben nodded toward Jack's hands, which were indeed wrapped around a spoon and fork as if they were drumsticks.

"Fair enough." Jack dropped his silverware and took a bite of his chip.

The back-and-forth between Jack and Ben continued for the rest of the period as they plotted our rise and subsequent fall from stardom. I was upset to hear that I was going to have a drug problem and Jack was going to bravely lead an intervention to save me. Which would be all for naught when, on the night before our big comeback tour, Ethan would tragically die in a car accident.

Jack shook his head sadly. "So much promise . . ."

As we all got up from our seats, Ethan finally spoke up. "What exactly happened just now?" he asked.

I shook my head. "I'm not entirely sure, but I believe we're in a band with Jack and Ben. Although you need to be sure to always wear a seat belt."

He smiled. "Oh, okay. You should stay away from the smack."

"I'll try."

"Cool."

Now, three years later, we're still talking about the future of our band.

"So nobody wants to hear what lies in store for us?" Jack pretends to be hurt. "You all want to throw away something we've worked so hard on?" He scrunches his face up like he's about to cry. "That's fine, that's fine."

Ben sighs. "Oh, you are such the martyr."

"Well, at least you understand my role." Jack wipes off his pretend tears with a napkin.

"Yeah, but if it wasn't for me, we'd still be called CPA Cliché."

Everybody at the table groans. For weeks we couldn't come up with a name for our band, and Jack had plenty. After we all vetoed CPA Cliché, we swiftly turned down Jack's other suggestions: Jack and the Irish (since the rest of us have Irish last names: Connelly, Quinn, and McWilliams), Black and the Irish (Jack's warped sense of humor), and his personal favorite, Jack and the Not-So-All-Star Band.

Ethan came up with Dissonance Youth, which we didn't think any non-music people would get. Ben and I were trying to come up with similarly obscure references, then suggested we just call the band Obscure Reference. Jack vetoed that. He didn't want there to be anything obscure about our band; he isn't into obscurity . . . or subtlety.

Then, as with everything about our band, our name sort of just came to us. Ethan started playing the opening chords of the Undertones' "Teenage Kicks" during rehearsal for our first gig and it just stuck. Teenage Kicks. We know that pigeonholes us as a teen band, but that's what we are.

The thought that this is our last year together makes me a little sad. I guess everybody is thinking the same thing, because Ben finally says, "Okay, what happens to us next, O wise one?"

Jack replies, "I've realized that I've been a little too hard on Red here." That's the understatement of the year. In every telling of our story, I end up with some horrible addiction . . . and Ethan dies tragically. Of course Jack becomes a huge star and Ben is some weird recluse who raises llamas or something. "I think you're going to like this one, Red."

I doubt it.

"We become instant sensations after we open for U2." Nobody bothers to ask how we went from CPA to opening for

U2, we just go with it. "Bono obviously becomes jealous of my dynamic personality and charisma."

"*Obviously*," Ben says with a dramatic rolling of the eyes.

"So he produces Jack and the Background Players —"

"Wait," Ben interrupts. "When did we get a new name and why on —"

"Hey! I'm telling a story here. So he produces *the band's* album and we become major stars. Soon U2 is opening for us. You know, because it's important to remember those little people who have helped you along the way. Soon tension begins in the band as the attention shifts from our beanpole of a lead singer —"

"Hey, I've gained some weight this summer, thank you very much," Ethan protests.

Jack gasps. "Yeah, you are probably what, a buck fifteen soaking wet? Big improvement."

I shake my head; the last thing we need to do is make Ethan even more self-conscious about his appearance. It took me two years to get him into jeans and T-shirts that actually fit. And then I swear he grew another six inches.

"Okay, so the attention shifts from our bulking stud of a lead singer to the magnetic drummer."

Ethan interrupts. "Yes, because that often happens with drummers." Jack glares at him. "But do go on. . . ."

"You're all obviously jealous of the attention I receive."

"*Obviously*," Ben and I say in unison.

"But things get even more complicated as Red realizes that Ben will never return her feelings for him."

"Um." I know better than to try to reason with him, but I try anyway. "Maybe the fact that Ben's gay has something to do with that?"

Jack nods at me with such sympathy. "But the heart, it wants what it wants."

"Sorry, Emme, this —" Ben gestures at me. "Not my thing."

Ethan begins to bang his head against the table. "Okay, we do have an audition next week, so can we please get on with this?"

Jack finally gives up. "Fine. I leave you all to become a ginormous star and marry an Oscar-winning actress-slash-Victoria's Secret model, while Ethan dies by getting hit by a bike messenger while busking outside a subway station, Ben goes to Montana to raise wild goats, and Red, to recover from her heartbreak over Ben's rejection, turns to her old friend Jack Daniel's. Happy?"

Ben claps. "That it's over? Yes."

"Wait, how exactly is this being easier on me?" I ask. "I still have an addiction and I'm miserable."

"You guys wanted the short version." Jack shrugs his shoulders and dives into his food.

Both Ben and Ethan glare at me, not wanting to prolong this any more.

"Plus" — Jack shoves a few fries into his mouth — "I thought it was best to make it short and sweet. We don't want Mount Saint Emme erupting again."

Ethan's fork drops, Ben looks down at the floor, and I just sit there with my mouth open. I can't believe Jack would bring up . . . The Incident.

Jack realizes, too late, what he's done. "You know, I . . ."

"Oh, so *now* you're at a loss for words?" Ethan says through clenched teeth. "Two seconds too late." He gets up to go to the bathroom.

"Emme . . ." Jack's voice is a low whisper.

"It's okay, it's not your fault. I'm the one . . ."

I don't even want to think about what happened this summer. Ethan and I haven't talked about it since. Nobody has.

I was hoping that we'd returned to normal. Things seemed to be a lot better.

However, Ethan's abrupt departure from the table makes it clear:

Appearances can be deceiving.

The following afternoon, Sophie knocks on my door.

"Greetings from Maryland!" She holds out something wrapped up in tissue paper.

"You remembered!" I take the gift and start to unwrap the tissue.

"Of course I remembered. I only do it every year."

It's a pink scallop seashell. "These are my favorite." I turn it over in my hand and rub the smooth surface.

Sophie shakes her head. "I can't believe you keep them. The first time I gave you one was because I was eight and cheap. What else do you give someone from the beach for free?" She glances over the other shells she's given me, all lined up on my bookshelf.

I place my newest shell next to the others. "It's not that."

"Right, it's the thought that counts."

"Stop it." I pick up the first one she gave me, a black-and-white shell. "I just think it's interesting to think about its journey. Where it's been, you know? It's probably traveled thousands of miles in the ocean and it ends up on a beach in Maryland."

"And then on some girl's bookshelf in Brooklyn. What a life!" She laughs. "Although I really shouldn't judge, since my journey hasn't been anything to brag about."

Sophie sits down on my bed and I see her study the photos on my wall. There's a collage of all the talent competitions Sophie and I have competed in. Sophie is wearing a blue ribbon or gold medal in all of them. But the photos stop when we're around fourteen. Our schedules at CPA don't really allow us to do much outside of school, and, well . . . Sophie really hasn't shone through as much as we thought she would.

She shakes her head, as if she's trying to get rid of whatever thought is there. "Sorry, I'm just in a crabby mood. Bad night."

"Oh, did you and Carter get into a fight or something?"

Sophie reaches into her bag and pulls out a stack of newspapers and printouts from online gossip columns. "No. I spent all last night posing for photographers and I was cut off in every picture except one." She hands me a spread from the Gossip Guru that has a picture of Sophie clutching on to Carter. "Carter Harrison and friend . . . *and friend*!"

I look at the photo. She has one arm wrapped around Carter,

while the other holds his hand. "It's pretty clear that you guys are a couple."

She picks up the photo and studies it. "That's not my point. I've been with Carter for two years now — shouldn't they recognize me already? And we're seniors now, so time is running out."

I know how much pressure senior year is going to be. I never thought it would get to Sophie, but she seems more stressed out than usual.

Sophie puts the articles back in her bag. "I really need my name out there. It's only a matter of time before I start working with talent scouts."

I don't say anything. I don't agree with Sophie's decision to avoid college and immediately dive into the world of Broadway and record contracts. It's not that I doubt her talent; it's just such a hard business.

"Anyway." Sophie lays her head on my shoulder. "I'm so sorry to dump that on you. How are things with the guys? Do you know what you're going to do for the audition?"

"Oh, it's fine. We're debating which of Ethan's songs to do." I feel a slight stab in my stomach as I say his name. When he returned to the table, we started talking about what songs to perform and mapped out a practice schedule. I tried to talk to him afterward, but he rushed off to the subway. I guess maybe it's better to let it go. I said my peace. Well, I said a lot of things. It was more like I was declaring war, but I had to do it.

"Hello?" Sophie waves her hand in front of my face. "Earth to Emme."

"Sorry."

She tilts her head. "Is everything all right?"

I nod. I'm glad to have Sophie back, and not just from Maryland, but back in my life. Each year it seems like she slips away from me. I know I carry the blame since I have to dedicate so much time to the band. But between homework, rehearsals, school performances, and band gigs, I don't have a lot of time for anything. Still, there will always be time for Sophie. We're a team. We're best friends.

I pull out the sheet music with my scribbles over it.

Sophie straightens up. "I've been warming up my voice. Tell me everything about it!"

"I've been working on this one idea for a while. It's about searching. The song is about searching for that person, the one who completes you. Sort of like 'Where are you already?' but I think it also works with where we are right now. Searching for our future, where we belong."

Sophie nods at me while she studies my lyrics. "Amazing, Emme. Really amazing."

I sit down at the keyboard in my room and begin to play the song for Sophie. After a few run-throughs, she begins to sing along. I love this stage of the writing process, when the song is like an intimate secret shared between us. It's a bond that can't be broken by school or by anyone. It's only the two of us.

After we practice for a while, I type out the reworked lyrics.

(Hearing Sophie sing always inspires me to make a few changes.) She hesitates before taking the sheet.

"Um, Em, I was hoping you could do me a huge favor." She begins to curl a long brunette strand of hair between her fingers. She does this when she waits for a callback list to be posted or when she thinks she's going to say something that will upset me.

I wish I wasn't so sensitive. I've never been tough like her. She's center stage. I'm background. That's just the way it has been and always will be.

She sits down next to me on the piano bench and grabs my hand. "I know how extremely busy you're going to be, and I was hoping you could write out the accompanying part so I could practice with Amanda."

"Oh." I try to not sound hurt. Amanda is a junior music student who has been practicing Sophie's other vocal department songs with her. But the songs I write have always been between the two of us.

"You know that Amanda is nowhere near the pianist that you are, but I really want to do well. It's senior year and it's hard for you and me to find the time with our schedules. You understand, don't you?"

What kind of friend would I be if I didn't give Sophie every advantage to nail her audition for the performance?

"Of course. I'll write it up tonight and send it to you."

"Oh, Emme." Sophie hugs me. "You're the greatest friend ever! I'm eternally indebted to you. You are so getting an entire paragraph in the liner notes for my first album. *To Emme, who has been my biggest supporter and friend since day one."*

I know that Amanda could never replace me. Really, when I think about it, she's helping me out. Senior year is going to be busy and I need to let go a little. I don't have the time and I can't do it all. If I keep trying to juggle everything, someone is going to end up getting shortchanged and I don't want to do that to Sophie and the guys, not to mention to my sanity.

After Sophie leaves, something registers in what she said. Her album. We used to discuss how I was going to write and produce her albums. But she hasn't said anything about me being part of her album in months.

Wow, Emme, needy much? I think.

Senior year hasn't even started, but I'm already worried about not being a part of an album that doesn't even exist yet.

I know how much I mean to Sophie. I've got to remember her Plan. I've always been part of it, a big part of it. And nothing will change that.

"I seriously can't believe you let her do that," Ethan whispers to me a week later at the auditions for the freshman welcome program. We're all lined up in the hallway waiting our turn.

I try to look content as I watch Sophie walk into her audition with Amanda. "She's been practicing the song more with Amanda than with me," I explain. "Do I need to remind you that I've been a little busy rehearsing with you guys?"

Jack stops twirling his drumsticks for a second. "Yeah, for two hours a day. You've got twenty-two other hours for Sophie. But apparently that isn't enough for the wanna-diva."

It's an argument we've had a lot. Ever since freshman year, there has been this pull on me between the guys and Sophie. Sophie thinks I spend too much time with them and they — well, they don't like her.

Ethan motions toward the door to the auditorium stage. "She's in there right now singing *your* song. Do you really think you're going to get the credit for it? You have to remember that this audition is also about you. *You* are being judged right now . . . if she even bothers to mention that it's one of your songs."

"She would never . . ." I know there's no way Sophie would take credit for the song. Everybody knows I write her songs. And she's been practicing with Amanda more than me, so am I supposed to punish her because *I'm* the one who's not available?

They don't get it. And they never have.

Ethan shakes his head. "She's already done the unforgivable, if you ask me."

"Yeah, well, I didn't ask."

Ben gets up and crouches next to us. "Hey, guys, we've got *our* audition coming up, so can we just concentrate on that, please?"

We both nod.

"Hey, Emme." Carter comes up to me. "Where's Sophie?"

I point to the door. "Oh," he says. "Why aren't you in there?"

Ethan gets up and walks away. Carter takes his seat.

"She's in with Amanda."

"Oh." Carter looks upset. "I'm sorry."

"It's okay."

He gives me a look that says *No, it's not*. And maybe it isn't, but there's nothing I can do about it now. Ben's right; I've got to get my head into our audition. *That* I can do something about.

I gesture toward the script rolled up in Carter's hand. "What are you doing?"

He looks at it. "Oh, I'm doing a monologue from *Death of a Salesman*, but this is the script for tomorrow's scene."

I don't know how Carter balances everything we do with school and acts in a soap opera at the same time. I know his mom worked out some arrangement so he only works about ten hours a week, but still.

He flips through the pages. "You don't even want to know what shenanigans Chase Proctor is up to now." He laughs and messes up his overly styled blond hair.

Oddly enough, I haven't really watched *Our Lives, Our Loves* since I've known him. Sophie was always obsessed with it, so I get updates every now and then about Carter's character, Chase Proctor, the good guy who turned bad after his parents got a divorce when his father started cheating with his mother's twin sister, who everybody thought was dead after she was trapped in a house that was set on fire by Chase's estranged grand-mother, who . . . oh, never mind.

Sophie and Amanda emerge from the audition, and Sophie heads straight for Carter. "You weren't here to wish me luck."

"But you don't need luck when you have a song by Emme," he says, grinning at me.

"Oh, hey, Emme!" Sophie gives me a big hug. "The song was great. I could tell they loved it." Amanda hangs behind her. She won't even talk to me. I don't know what she has against me since we've only ever exchanged a handful of words in the past. She's the only junior here, so she should show me some grati-tude for being such an unreliable friend that it got her into the audition.

I debate thanking her for helping out, but then I hear our names being called. "Emme Connelly, Jack Coombs, Benjamin McWilliams, and Ethan Quinn."

"Good luck, Emme," Carter calls out. I turn my back on them just as I hear Sophie reply, "Sure, you wish *her* luck."

Ethan can tell something's wrong. He grabs me by the shoul-der. "Please don't do this right now."

I look at him. "Do what?"

"Question yourself, your friendship, whether you belong here. Because you do belong here. You're one of the best stu-dents here. I know it, the teachers know it, everybody knows it. *She* knows it. I wish you did."

He walks to the center of the stage, picks up a guitar, and pulls the microphone stand up to match his height. Jack goes behind the kit while Ben grabs the bass. I stand there for a second before I instinctively pick up the other guitar and stand to Ethan's left.

This stage, one I used to admire as a kid going to CPA productions, is so familiar to me now. But what I feel isn't familiar. Usually I get nervous doing the walk from the hallway to the stage to audition each semester. But this time I don't feel nerves at all. Because I'm with the guys. I don't get nervous performing with them. Sure, I used to, but we're a team, a musical family. We've grown up together.

"Hello, we're Teenage Kicks and we'll be performing an original song that I wrote," Ethan says into the microphone.

I remember the first time we performed together. Ethan wouldn't even look out into the audience, let alone speak to them. He stared down at the floor the entire time. I'm not sure he's ever forgiven us for making him be the lead singer, but he has the most incredible voice. The second we heard him sing, we knew we had our front man.

He turns back and looks at each one of us. When he gets to me, he asks, "Ready?"

I'm not sure how prepared I am for senior year, the showcase, and college applications, but in this moment, I know that with these three guys behind me, I can do anything.

I look at him and smile. "Ready."

CARTER

e're about to find out who made the cut. I can see the tension in all the students walking into CPA. Everybody but me. It's not like I'm some hugely confident person, but I've been dealing with rejection like this for so long, it's not even a big deal to me.

But it is to Sophie.

She squeezes my hand as we ascend the stairs.

> SOPHIE: I don't know if I can handle another year of this. I mean, I *need* this, you know?

She leans against the wall near the entrance. I brush a loose piece of hair from her face. Sophie's been a nervous wreck since the auditions. I study her and wonder what happened to that super-confident girl who approached me sophomore year and straight-up asked me out. At that point, all I got was glares from the students. Half of them hated me because they thought I was a hack and would recite my infamous *Kavalier Kids* line, "Anytime a stranger is in need, the Kavalier Kids will be there, indeed!" as I walked down the hallways. The other half despised me for landing every lead role and getting all the press.

But Sophie was the first person to show me an ounce of kindness. She treats me like a normal guy. She's put up with my crazy schedule, public appearances, and fans (who do *not* appreciate me having a girlfriend). She was also there for me when I was starting to doubt a lot of things.

It probably started the night of the *Inside the Outside* premiere — I wasn't in the movie, but I was invited to decorate the occasion. Not quite Oscar night, but there's still a red carpet and a long line of reporters to deal with before you're allowed to take your seat and watch the movie. (Most premieres aren't even about the movie; it's about being *seen* on the red carpet or at the after-party.)

The lights were flashing so quickly, and I could barely focus with the paparazzi screaming my name over and over again. Sophie patiently waited off camera with my publicist, Sheila Marie.

Sophie and I had only been dating a couple months, but she'd been nothing but supportive of everything. In fact, she made me want to go out and do this sort of thing more. It's a lot less lonely when you have someone to go with . . . who isn't your mom.

REPORTER: Carter! Over here!

I headed over to a petite blond reporter for an entertainment program, flashing a smile.

REPORTER: Great to see you here, Carter. How have you enjoyed the transition from child star to high school student? What year are you now?

ME: I'm in the first semester of my sophomore year at the New York City High School of the Creative and Performing Arts. It's been a really great learning experience not to mention being a ton of fun.

REPORTER: That's great. Tell us, how do you feel about the recent Gossip Guru article about the *Kavalier Kids* curse?

I stared at her blankly. I had no idea what she was talking about. I generally ignore those tabloid rags.

REPORTER: Did you really go to school because the roles dried up?

What?

ME: I'm on *Our Lives* . . .

REPORTER: Yes, but that's a soap.

Sheila Marie quickly grabbed me by the arm.

SHEILA MARIE: Interview's over. He's got to be inside.

Sheila Marie guided Sophie and me inside to a private corner.

ME: What's going on? What is she talking about?

SHEILA MARIE: I told them not to bring up that vile article.

ME: What article? What's going on?

SHEILA MARIE: Your mother thought it would be best if you didn't see it, but there was this ridiculous article that came out that featured the kids from the series. And, well, not everything has turned out well for you guys. And honestly, you do come off the best, but they . . .

ME: What did it say?

I felt sick to my stomach. This definitely wasn't the first time I'd had a negative article about me in the press. It had started after I'd had my first box office dud — I was eleven and being told that my career was over. I was "box office poison" simply because a comedy about me and a talking dog bombed. It wasn't like I wrote or directed it, but it was my face on the poster, so the studio decided to blame the kid.

But this was different. These were my choices. Yes, I knew that I'd get made fun of for being on a soap, but that was the only thing I could think of that would allow me to still work and go to school.

Sheila Marie pulled up the article on her phone. I started reading about the other actors that I'd worked with — guys I grew up with — who'd been kicked out of school, busted for DUI, arrested for stealing, or had run away. Of course, they didn't mention the other three guys, who were now just normal high school students.

And then there was me. I got my own box, where they dissected my meteoric rise in one paragraph and then spent the next dozen recounting every small role I'd taken since. They belittled my choice to go to CPA, calling it "desperate," my "last chance to redeem" myself.

I didn't believe my own press when I was called the next big thing, but it's harder when they're calling you a failure.

SHEILA MARIE: I'm going to call your mom. I'm so sorry — we should've told you.

ME: It's okay. It's not like I haven't heard it before.

I walked into the theater and did my best to smile at the other attendees. We were guided to our seats and Sophie offered to sit on the aisle so nobody could bother me. Sheila Marie went off to make a phone call. I knew she didn't have control over what they said. I wasn't mad at her. Strangely, I was more mad at myself. Because some of the article rang true. And I could imagine my fellow students reading the article and believing every word.

I may be a former child star and have millions in my bank account, but I'm still a human being.

SOPHIE: Carter . . .

She took my hand and leaned in so nobody could hear her.

SOPHIE: I know this isn't the same, but I used to be a big deal back in Brooklyn, before CPA. People actually followed me around the hallways and asked for my autograph at school events. Everybody thought I was going to be a huge star, and so did I. Then I got to CPA and nobody would turn around when I came down a hallway. I wasn't special, I was normal. It was really hard to take at first. It's not fun to be called a has-been, but you've shined brighter than most people could ever dream of. And honestly, I think that only the best is yet to come. For both of us. You've handled it all so well. You're still a working actor, you're one of the nicest guys I've ever known, and um, a really good kisser.

.   She smiled and gave me a soft kiss on the cheek.

SOPHIE: At the end of the day, I don't think I've ever met anybody as special and deserving of their dreams as you.

I look at Sophie now. With each passing semester, her confidence gets stripped away. I do my best to comfort her; we both know what it's like to not be the big star you once were. But lately, she's become too desperate for the limelight. She's not the person I fell for, the one who would light up a room simply by entering it. Instead, she walks into a room and takes stock of the competition. Now everything seems like a big battle to her.

I want the old Sophie back.

ME: I have no doubt in my mind that you are going to land a spot.

I wrap my arms around her to try to give her some comfort. She holds on to me tight.

SOPHIE: It's our last year. I've got to start making an impression or . . . Plus, it isn't even about making the list, it's the *order*, too.

I don't know what to say. I couldn't care less about the order. But I know, to her, it's everything.

She sighs, grabs my hand, and leads me inside the building.

> SOPHIE: This is really the first test to see who the lead contenders for the Senior Showcase are. There are ten spots. The first spot is a big deal because that sets the tone. But then spots two through eight are fine. The second to the last is pretty major, but the last spot — that's the cream of the crop.

I nod like I have any clue what she's talking about. I know she's nervous about the lineup and I want to be there for her, but senior year has made me realize that I have my own issues, too. I thought going to high school would give me some sort of sense of who I really am. But it's just another part I'm playing. And now I'm playing the role of Understanding Boyfriend.

Still, having a girlfriend at school is one of the things that makes me feel normal. Plus, she's superhot.

It's not that I don't want to play the boyfriend role, but I guess there's no denying there's been some tension between us lately. She's become so obsessed with being the biggest star at CPA, it's getting in the way of our relationship. When she's not worried about an audition, she's a ton of fun, and she likes to be out and be seen (something Mom wants me to do for my career — be in papers, online, TV, you name it. Got to stay relevant, I guess). Although sometimes I get the feeling that it's an act to her, too.

> SOPHIE: Did you hear that Zach did a monologue
> from *Richard III*?

I groan. I know Sophie, and everybody else for that matter, probably thinks my attitude is because Zachary David is the other lead student in the drama department and we are always competing for roles, but he's the one who considers me competition, not vice versa. My disgust is over my real nemesis: Shakespeare. That guy kills me. I get why he's a big deal, I really do. But it's hard to memorize pages and pages of something that makes zero sense. And did people ever really talk like that?

But *of course* Zach auditioned with Shakespeare. He's by far the better actor, one of the best I've ever seen. I'm aware that I'm not even in the top half of the class, but I always seem to get the lead. Which pisses everybody off. And it should. I know why I get the lead parts — it's because any production I'm in sells out. It's all about the money, and my name equals tween girls and their moms. A school like CPA requires a lot of funding for costumes, sets, instruments, etc. And "Carter Harrison" still sells tickets.

Although I don't think my acting does anything for the school's reputation.

We find some seats in the auditorium and wait for our fates. You could hear a pin drop as Dr. Pafford takes the stage and gets right to what we are all here for.

> DR. PAFFORD: The following is the order of the performances for Monday's assembly. If your name isn't called, please exit the auditorium and have a good weekend. First up, Sarah Moffitt singing "Somewhere" from *West Side Story*.

Sophie growls at the mere mention of Sarah's name. Sarah is *her* nemesis.

> DR. PAFFORD: Up next, I will be combining two performances. The string quartet of Collins, Hoffman, McDonnell, and Shannon will perform Vivaldi while the art of Trevor Parsons is displayed overhead.

Trevor's an amazing artist. I go to all his openings. I love to draw — I love it more than acting — and he's been an inspiration to me. Although I don't think I could ever show anybody my art. My art is the only thing that I feel truly belongs to me. It would be too difficult to open myself up that way.

> DR. PAFFORD: Sophie Jenkins will perform an original song by Amanda Jones.

SOPHIE (quietly): I'm *third*? Are you kidding me?

I find it odd that her first reaction isn't mine. That song is Emme's. I try to catch Emme's eye from across the room, but she's looking straight ahead, her face bright red. I'm good at reading people (been doing it forever) and it's clear she's about ready to cry. Meanwhile, Ethan, Ben, and Jack look like they're about to commit a murder. I wish I had friends who would stick up for me like that.

The list of performers continues and we reach the final three.

DR. PAFFORD: Zachary David will be performing from *Richard III*, followed by Connelly, Coombs, McWilliams, and Quinn performing an original song by Ethan Quinn. Finally, we'll close out with Carter Harrison.

I hear the collective dissent in the room. After we get further instructions on the performance, we're excused, and I think it's probably best to leave, more for Sophie's safety than for my own.

I see Jack approach us. He usually has a permanent smile on his face, but not today.

JACK: Congrats, guys. That's really great. Great.

It's pretty obvious he doesn't think it's great.

JACK: Hey, Sophie, I didn't know you weren't performing Emme's song.

SOPHIE: What? Yes, I am.

JACK: Really? Did you bother telling anybody?

SOPHIE: What are you talking about?

Emme approaches us, with Ethan and Ben right behind her. I wonder if she knows how lucky she is to have such supportive friends.

JACK: Did you not hear who they gave the song credit to?

SOPHIE: To be honest, I was a little shocked that my name was only called third.

EMME: Hey, guys, it's fine. Just a mistake.

Ethan is glaring at Sophie. Ben looks like he's prepared to break up a fight.

EMME: It's fine, really. I'll be performing it with her on Monday, so there won't be any confusion. Sophie, why don't you come over tomorrow so we can practice?

SOPHIE: What are you guys even talking about?

JACK: Pafford said Amanda wrote the song.

Sophie seems to come out of her trance.

SOPHIE: Oh, no, I didn't hear. I was so upset over not being in the second half. I'm so sorry, Emme. I really don't know what happened, honestly.

Sophie hugs Emme. And everything seems to be right with them. It always is.

EMME: Don't worry about it. Hey, we're playing at Kat's Café tonight if you guys want to come.

I've only seen Teenage Kicks perform at school events. I've always wanted to see them outside of CPA.

ME: Really? That's great. What time?

Everybody turns around. Probably shocked that I'm speaking. I usually don't say much. I'm better if something is scripted out for me.

EMME: Eight. We're testing out some new stuff. It would be really great if you guys came.

SOPHIE: We'll see.

We'll see? I know Sophie's upset, but I want to go. I want to have fun this year. Make friends.

I'm seventeen years old. It's about time I stop pretending and just figure it out already.

I get to the television studio after having an argument with Sophie about our evening plans. She wants me to call Sheila Marie to see if she can get us into any events. But I'm going to the concert. She can do whatever she wants.

I open up the script for today's scene and start to draw.

Mom enters the room, her own copy of the script in hand.

MOM: Carter, fabulous news, sweetheart! I just got out of
a meeting with Timothy and big things are happening.

I hate it when Mom talks to the show runner. She's always trying to get me bigger dramatic moments and what she usually ends up doing is making me seem like a big brat.

MOM: What your story line needs is for Chase to
come to terms with his feelings for Charity.

She looks so serious, like these are real people. Chase is certainly not a real person. In fact, he's getting so out there, I don't even know how to play him anymore. Not like I ever really liked playing him. But I sometimes get the feeling that Mom thinks that *I'm* Chase.

Mom starts to clap, mostly to get my attention, because it's clear that I couldn't care less about Chase and Charity.

MOM: Today you'll be filming your first love scene!

Great. Mom's probably convinced that if Charity and Chase get romantically involved, it'll get me more screen time. The original agreement was that when I'm attending CPA, the producers have to reduce the number of scenes that I have each week so I can go to school full-time. But that hasn't really happened.

Most parents would want their children to focus on their studies. But I learned a long time ago that my mother isn't like most parents.

Mom sits down next to me on the couch and places her hand on my knee.

MOM: Honey, I'm so sorry. I completely spaced. How did the lineup for the freshman assembly go?

ME: I got in. Last slot.

MOM: And that's good, right? The last slot, like the headliner, or am I getting that mixed up?

I remember what Sophie told me.

ME: It's good.

MOM: Oh, Carter. That's wonderful. I'm so proud of
you. I . . . Did you eat lunch?

She rummages through her purse to give me a protein bar.
My diet has been a serious topic lately since the producers feel
the need for my character to appear shirtless. *A lot.* Because
most seventeen-year-old guys hang out at home in khakis and
nothing else. In one scene, I take off my shirt before I open up a
book. I don't get it, but apparently the viewers like it. It's beyond
embarrassing.

So I'm on a high-protein diet to bulk up. And I've got to work
out more. Just more things to add to the list of things I have no
interest in doing.

Although Sophie really likes it.

MOM: I know what this is about. Honey, I know that
having your first on-screen love scene can be stressful
and you've known Charity, I mean Britney, for years
and she's like a sister to you, but it isn't a big deal. Just
think of that cute Sophie girl and everything will
be fine.

She gets up and leaves without even waiting for a reply. It
wouldn't matter anyway. The decision has been made.

★　★　★　★　★　★　★　★　★　★　★　★　★　★

There's a line outside of Kat's when I arrive, alone, around seven thirty. As I scan the line, I can't tell if these kids are from school or not. I knew the band was getting a reputation outside CPA but didn't know they were this big.

"Carter?" I turn around to find Chloe Nagano, Jack's girlfriend. Even outside of school, you can tell she's a dancer. Her hair is up in a bun and she's got a tight tank top on with leggings, and a sweater wrapped around her waist.

CHLOE: I was just heading inside to say hi to Jack. Is Sophie with you?

ME: No, I came by myself.

CHLOE: Oh. Well, it's just me here, too. Do you want to join me?

I follow Chloe behind an alley to the back entrance of the coffee shop/music venue. The band is crammed in a tiny space that I guess is supposed to be the greenroom. Emme's doing homework, Ethan's running in place, and Ben and Jack are arguing about some band I've never heard of.

They all look up when I enter the room.

JACK: There's my girl.

Jack gets up to kiss Chloe. I stand there awkwardly, wondering what they all think of me, especially after what happened today. Death by association? Sophie said it was an honest mistake and Emme didn't seem to have a problem, but these guys . . . well, it's pretty obvious they don't like Sophie.

Emme smiles warmly at me.

EMME: Hey, Carter! Is Sophie with you?

ME: No, she couldn't make it. But I've really wanted to see you guys perform.

JACK: Well, I don't mean to brag. . . .

BEN: Yes, he does.

JACK: You're in for a treat. We're on for an hour today, which should mean . . . three songs with the way this one's been blabbing on recently.

He points to Ethan, who is now doing jumping jacks.

JACK: At first we couldn't get the guy to talk, and now he won't shut up.

ETHAN: One time. *One time* I talked too much.

The other three members roll their eyes collectively.

JACK: Yeah, okay, one time. Sure, sure. Tell me, Carter, have you ever wondered what the origin of the word *fan* is?

I shake my head.

JACK: Well, if you do, Ethan over there has about a half-hour description. Which would be fascinating . . . if you were in an insane asylum.

CHLOE: Well, we just came to say hi. I want to grab our table before someone takes it. Good luck, guys!

I don't really know what to say, so I just wave good-bye. Chloe links her arm with mine as we make our way through the crowded room.

CHLOE: Tonight is going to be interesting. Ethan can be a bit of a loose cannon. It's funny, they used to have to beg him to even address the audience, and now he won't shut up. It just depends on the day, I guess. His behavior has been a little unpredictable and tonight is their first big gig since —

Chloe stops herself and studies a flyer.

CHLOE: You know, it's Friday, so I'm allowed a treat.
I'm getting a brownie, do you want anything?

I think about my diet: protein, protein, and more protein. But if Chloe, whose profession is even more weight-conscious than acting, can treat herself, why can't I?

ME: Yeah, a brownie sounds great. But here, let me
get it.

I hand her a twenty as she flags down somebody she knows to get our brownies before we settle down at a table up front with her name on it. The place is so packed, our table is right up against the side of the stage. I can literally rest my arm on one of the speakers. Chloe grabs our chocolate fixes and cuts hers into tiny pieces.

CHLOE: I'm glad I ran into you. I used to have Kelsey
to keep me company, but she's no longer in the picture.

I raise my eyebrow since my mouth is full of the most amazing brownie I've ever tasted.

CHLOE: Oh, Kelsey used to be Ethan's girlfriend.
They'd been going out for years, but it was such a

dysfunctional relationship. They'd go out, he'd write these amazing love songs about her. But then she wouldn't be at a show and these girls would throw themselves at him because of songs he wrote about Kelsey. He'd cheat, and then he'd write some song begging for forgiveness. She'd take him back and it would all repeat.

ME: Really?

I always saw Ethan as this quiet guy. He was usually with someone from the band, so I always took him as a pretty loyal guy. Guess not.

CHLOE: Yeah, it got to be ridiculous. Get back together, cheat, fight, get back together, rinse, and repeat. He was so annoying to be around. Always sulking about his love life. He even started to drink before the shows. Finally, Emme lost it on him.

ME: Emme?

Chloe laughs.

CHLOE: I know, right? Emme is the sweetest thing. But from the way Jack tells it, she totally lost her mind on him. Started screaming at him to stop being such a . . . I think it was "a self-sabotaging moron" or something. I can't remember her exact words, but the whole incident really shook up the band. They didn't hear from Ethan for two weeks, and when he came back, he said he'd ended his relationship with Kelsey for good and he wasn't going to drink anymore, period. No one really believes him.

ME: About the drinking or Kelsey? Don't they like her?

CHLOE: No, he hasn't had anything to drink or anything, but with Kelsey it's not like they didn't like her. They *really* liked her. I don't think any of them could take how he treated her. Especially Emme. Although the weird thing is that Kelsey wasn't a fan of Emme's.

I find that hard to believe. Who could find anything wrong with Emme? She's so nice . . . and probably too loyal a friend.

CHLOE: Emme made every effort, but I don't think Kelsey liked Ethan's relationship with Emme.

ME: Did they ever?

CHLOE: God, no. Emme and Ethan are really close — or at least they used to be. Ethan clearly adores Emme and is very protective of her. I don't think Kelsey appreciated that. I know Emme thinks Sophie is her best friend, but it's really Ethan and the guys who have her back. She's just so blinded by that girl. No offense.

ME: None taken.

The lights go down and the place erupts in cheers and applause.

Jack gets behind his drum kit while Ben and Emme plug in their guitars. Ethan comes storming onto the stage with his hands up. The girls start screaming for him.

It's funny because Ethan doesn't really make any impact at school. Sure, he's known as one of the best music students, but he doesn't grandstand or walk around demanding attention like most of the top students at CPA. He seems to enjoy flying under the radar, but up onstage, he commands attention. His charisma is palpable and I can now understand why there are so many girls here.

The band starts playing a song I've never heard before, one of their originals. But the people jammed up front are singing along to every word.

It's amazing to see them up onstage. Seeing them walking down the street or even in a cramped greenroom, I don't think you'd stop and think that these four people belong together. Jack: big teddy bear with a full head of wild Afro curls.

Ben: unassuming dirty-blond-haired, blue-eyed guy who just happily strums his bass. Ethan: tall (he's got to be close to six foot three now) and skinny, his black hair a little long and a bit curly; Emme: with her bright red hair, pale freckled skin, wearing all black and bobbing to the music as she strums her guitar.

But even if they look different, together onstage they're a complete unit. It isn't their friendship that I envy the most; it's the passion for what they're doing right at this moment. It's clear that each one of them loves playing music. It's their calling. It's what they want to do.

Chloe leads me backstage after the concert. We get stopped a few times on the way for some photos, which I oblige. During the entire concert, I felt like a normal student watching his friends play. But once the lights came on, I saw all the girls with their cameras out, waiting for a picture. I was hoping "Carter Harrison" could take the night off. And the last thing I want to do is take any attention away from the band. Tonight is about them.

We get into the small room, which has become even tighter with people. Several girls have made their way backstage, all fighting for Ethan's attention. The rest of the band are putting their instruments away. Chloe immediately finds Jack and, once again, I'm standing there trying to look like I belong.

Emme spots me and makes her way over. A few girls back up so Emme is intentionally pushed. She doesn't seem to realize it, or maybe she's used to it by now.

EMME: Hey, Carter, thanks for coming.

I stumble over my words for a moment and then it hits me, what I want to say. Actually, what I want to know.

ME: Do you love what you do?

If Emme is taken by surprise with this abrupt question, she doesn't show it.

EMME: Yes. Performing used to make me so nervous, but not with these guys.

ME: You were really amazing. Truly. I love the new songs and the covers. Everything. I can't believe four people can make such a complete sound.

I know that sounds stupid, but Emme blushes anyway.

EMME: Thanks.

I don't know what it is (maybe the chocolate?), but suddenly I feel like I can tell Emme anything. Like she'll understand me. I want to open up to somebody.

ME: Hey, can I buy you, like, a coffee or something? I'd love to talk to you some more, unless . . .

I don't know if they have other plans or she's tired or what. I see Ethan studying me. He comes over and gives Emme a hug.

ETHAN: Great show tonight.

EMME: Thanks. I'm going to pack up and then head out with Carter. Do you want me to grab your cords onstage so you can get back to your fan club?

Emme moves her chin subtly over to the group of four girls glaring at her.

Ethan doesn't even turn around to acknowledge them.

ETHAN: No, it's okay. I'll go with you.

A girl comes over and tugs Ethan's shirt.

GIRL: Hey, Ethan, I totally want to show you the pictures I took.

I can tell Ethan has no interest in looking at the girl's photos. I can also sense tension between Ethan and Emme.

ME: I can help pack up and, like, move stuff or whatever.

Very elegant, Carter.

EMME: That'd be great, thanks.

Emme moves to leave the room, and Ethan pulls away from the other girl and grabs Emme's arm.

ETHAN: Just give me a few minutes and I can help.

Emme shakes her head.

EMME: It's getting late, and I want to pack up and leave. You know, some of us do have a curfew. Don't worry about it — we can handle the breakdown. Talk to you later.

Emme turns on her heel and walks out the door. I follow her down the hallway, onto the stage.

Jack and Ben are already there disassembling the drum kit and amps. Jack doesn't hesitate putting me to work. And I love it. I mean, I realize that I'm here purely for manual labor, but being with them makes me feel like part of the team.

I'm a little disappointed when the last amp is packed into the truck.

Ethan comes out to the alley with two girls following behind him.

JACK: Nice for you to show up once we're done.

Ethan clenches his teeth and ignores the laughter coming from the two girls leaning against the wall.

EMME: Okay, guys, I'm heading out. Great show.

Emme gives each of the guys a hug. After she embraces Ethan, he leans in and whispers something in her ear. She turns around with an annoyed look on her face.

Emme leads me to a place close to the F train. She gets a green tea while I get a delicious mocha drink (if I'm going to splurge, might as well do it big-time, right?).

I go on and on about the show, and Emme listens patiently as she sips her tea. I run out of compliments and after I use the word *awesome* for the twelfth time, I decide to take a break.

EMME: You know, Carter, it's okay. You can talk to me about Sophie.

ME: Sophie?

Sophie hasn't even entered my mind the entire evening. Which should probably give me a hint of how well things are going between us.

EMME: Yeah, I assumed that's what you wanted to talk to me about.

Oh, of course she assumed that it was about Sophie. This was a stupid idea.

ME: No, I just . . .

She sets her glass down and leans in. Her bright green eyes sparkle, and I can tell that I can trust her. Sophie constantly says what a good friend she is, and it's clear that Emme has always gone out of her way for her friends.

ME: Actually, I wanted to talk to you about school.
And I know this is going to sound weird, but this
isn't how I thought school would be.

She nods at me knowingly. I can tell that she is going to let me talk. I'm not used to that. Mom and Sophie do the talking. I do the listening. But not tonight. Tonight I'm going to say what I've been dying to scream out for years.

ME: I hate acting.

There. I've said it. And now I feel the floodgates open.

ME: Acting wasn't even my choice. I've been doing it
for forever and I don't even like it. Sure, as a kid it was
like playing pretend. And I had fun traveling the world

and doing the *Kavalier Kids* movies, but then it just became so redundant. We sat around, got tutored, spent four hours shooting three lines of dialogue. At least with the soap, everything moves quickly because we've got five hours of TV to fill a week. But I'm not happy. This isn't what I want. I don't know what I want.

I pause.

ME: Actually, that's a lie. I love to draw and paint. I love art. Sometimes on the weekends, I put on a baseball hat and a hoodie and spend hours at galleries in SoHo. And that's such a stupid thing to have to hide. But I hide it from my mom, who wants me to return to the glory days. I know she'd think there's no future in art, but like there is in acting? Let's face it, I'm not that good. Sure, as a kid, I got by being all cute, but I don't have the desire or depth to do more adult roles. I get the lead in everything because the girls will buy the tickets. Most of the teachers don't even like me. Let's not even get into the students. I don't know. And I don't know why I'm babbling to you, I just . . . I see you up onstage with the guys and you seem happy. Like you're doing exactly what you are meant to do. Do you have any idea what a blessing that is? I don't even see you that happy when you're performing with Sophie.

I know I've hit a nerve. I can see her shift uncomfortably.

ME: I'm sorry, I know that is none of my business. I just . . . I want to be happy.

I finally let out a breath and take a sip of my mocha.

EMME: What would make you happy? Right now.

ME: Quitting the soap.

EMME: Okay.

She says it like that is so easy. But I guess it is. Money isn't an issue. I technically don't have to work.

EMME: And then?

ME: Take art classes.

EMME: Okay. So you need to quit the soap and take art classes.

Quit the soap and take art classes.

EMME: Does your mom have any idea about how you feel?

I shake my head. This has been her dream for so long, I don't think she's ever taken a moment to consider what *I* want.

> ME: No, I've been keeping everything hidden from
> her. I don't think she'd take it well.

> EMME: But this is *your* life.

Yes, my life. Carter Harrison. Not "Carter Harrison" the all-American, blond-haired (thanks, lemon juice!), blue-eyed, sparkly white-teeth (thanks, bleach!) act. Me. Plain Carter. I hesitate as I want to tell her more, but I figure trying to quit the soap will be hard enough. So I'll talk to Mom about quitting the soap and taking art classes.

Yeah, that's going to be fun.

> EMME: Can I see your art?

Even though Emme has told me to basically flip my world upside down, this is what scares me the most.

> ME: I've never shown anybody my art. I don't
> know, this is going to seem stupid, but it feels too
> personal.

Emme nods her head.

EMME: I know exactly what you're saying. I feel that way about my songs sometimes. But for me it's easy — Sophie is the one who gets up there and sings my words. It actually helps me when I'm writing the lyrics. I don't have to censor myself, wondering if people will read into something, because I know it won't be me up there singing it. I kind of see Sophie as my security blanket. I guess artists don't have that luxury.

I never thought of it like that before. That Emme, who has this incredible support system, would feel self-conscious about her songs. And I never realized how much *she* needs Sophie. I always saw it from Sophie's perspective, that Sophie needs Emme's songs.

I guess we're both hiding in our own ways.

ME: Well, I'm going to have to show it to people sometime. Although I do need to warn you, I'm no Trevor Parsons.

EMME: Trevor had to start somewhere. You know, he would be a great person to talk to.

I laugh. Emme makes this all seem so simple. But maybe it is. It can't be any harder than keeping a straight face saying lines like "Dammit, Charity, I'm not a mind reader, I'm just a guy trying to tell you how I feel inside!"

I think about my conversation with Emme as I go for a run in Central Park the next morning. Running helps clear my head, and I need it for what awaits me at home. I come back to our Central Park West apartment to find Mom at the kitchen table, reading scripts for me.

MOM: Honey, I made you some eggs.

I go to the counter, scoop up the eggs, and pour myself a glass of orange juice.

MOM: No juice — too much sugar.

I sit down and don't say anything.

MOM: Nervous about school on Monday?

I shake my head. Nope, not nervous about that. Although about the conversation I want to have right now? I believe *terrified* is the word I'm thinking of.

ME: I need to talk to you.

She puts down the script and removes her reading glasses.

ME: It's about the soap. I don't want —

MOM: I know, honey, and I'm so sorry about the pressure the producers have been putting on you for the new Charity story line. At first, I thought it would help with school starting, they know your hours are being cut and I think they wanted to give you something big before you wouldn't be around so much.

ME: It's not that. I don't want to do it anymore.

MOM: I'm confused. You don't want to do the Charity story line or the show?

ME: The show.

MOM: Oh.

She looks down at the table and nods.

MOM: Okay, Carter. But you do realize you're on a contract.

What is going on? She's so calm. This isn't what I was expecting; this isn't how she reacts when I . . .

I try to think about a time when I stood up for myself and

said I didn't want to go on an audition or accept a role. And I can't. That's impossible. I . . .

ME: How long is the contract for?

MOM: Just until next September.

Next September? That's a year.

MOM: Let me talk to the producers and see what we can do. We'll work something out, but you won't be able to quit right away.

I shake my head. That's it. She's not going to . . .

To what? I start going through all the scenarios in my head of when I've taken roles, and it's always been my decision. I'm the one who put myself in this circumstance. *I'm* the one who thought a soap would be a good way to balance school.

MOM: I'm glad you said something to me, honey. I didn't know you were that unhappy with the show, but you've been demonstrating so much promise at school, it makes sense you'd want to concentrate on your senior year.

I'm in shock. I quietly eat the rest of my eggs as I try to even think about what must be going through her mind.

Mom hands me the script she's been reading.

>MOM: I think this is really good; you should read it.
>Tell me what you think. Maybe you can do this next?

She kisses me on the cheek and pats my back before she heads to the living room.

I'm so shocked that I don't even bring up art. No point doing that until I know what's going on with the show.

I clean the dishes in a daze. Then I automatically pick up the script she handed me and head to my room. Anything to take my mind off what will happen once I stop acting, once I don't have a role to hide behind.

So the question is: Am I really ready to be just plain old Carter?

On Monday, while the rest of the school begins classes, the selected performers wait backstage as Dr. Pafford does his usual scaring of the freshman class. Reminding them that while they were probably the top music/art/dance/drama students in whatever borough they came from, they are average here. That on top of academics, they've got four studio classes. That they are here for an hour longer than "normal" high schools.

Emme approaches me with a smile on her face. I told her about my conversation with my mom and she was really happy. Sophie, on the other hand, can't believe that I'd want to leave the show.

It isn't until after Emme gives me a hug that I notice that Trevor Parsons is behind her.

EMME: Hey, Carter, do you know Trevor?

TREVOR: Hey, man. I, of course, know who you are.

I shake his hand and can hardly speak. I've been around a bunch of celebrities in my life, but there's something about Trevor that renders me utterly speechless.

EMME: I've been talking to Trevor about possibly doing some artwork for the band.

ME: Cool.

Cool? This is not the impression I want to make with somebody like Trevor.

EMME: I hope you don't mind, Carter, but I was telling Trevor about how you've been doing some of your own art, and how I thought that maybe he could give you some pointers.

TREVOR: Can totally do that. I love seeing other people's work. And seeing anything that's being done outside these walls would be a welcome sight. Here, let me give you my number.

This really is a lot simpler than I thought. What was my excuse all this time for continuing to do something that makes me unhappy?

Emme stands back and watches as Trevor and I exchange information. I want to run over, pick her up, and give her a hug.

But there isn't time. The cue comes up and we all take our places. Over the next thirty minutes or so, the new class is treated to performances from my peers. They shine onstage because it's what they love. They are CPA's finest.

And then there's me.

I've wanted to blame my mom for the position I'm in, but her reaction made me realize that maybe she wasn't the one pushing me this entire time.

I never once complained about being an actor. About going on auditions.

This was all on me.

As I take to the stage, a line from *Death of a Salesman* comes into my mind. Not from the part I'm going to be performing, but from Willy Loman's son, Biff.

I look out into the audience and hear the screaming from the girls. Those words echo loudly in my head.

I realized what a ridiculous lie my whole life has been.

ETHAN

*T*here is one thing I can say with certainty: I am not anywhere near the worst disaster at the freshman performance. Far from it. That honor belongs to one Carter Harrison.

We file into our first studio class for music composition after the performances. "Well, we've always known he hasn't gotten by on his *talent*," Jack says as he takes his usual seat in the back row.

"Be nice," Emme scolds as she sits in front of him. Ben sits next to Jack, and I sit in front of him, next to Emme. This is pretty much how it's been since freshman year.

"Plus," she continues, "he's been going through a lot. So he botched a few lines — that's happened to all of us." She looks directly at me.

Okay, she has a point, but Jack isn't one to back down.

"How would you know what's going on with him?"

Yeah, why does Emme know anything about Carter's life? Like one after-concert talk makes them lifelong friends. It's not as if Sophie would ever dare discuss anything that didn't revolve around her.

"Just drop it." She turns toward the front of the class, waiting for Mr. North to start.

The other students quickly file in and take the remaining seats. The music composition program started with eighteen students. Now there are only twelve of us left.

"Welcome, seniors!" Mr. North greets us as he walks in, sleeves rolled up, like he's ready to dive into whatever challenge he places in front of us. "I won't delay the torture any longer." A nervous giggle echoes in the large studio room. "We've done style analysis, composing for vocal, small form, and full orchestra. This year, the focus will be on contemporary arrangement and productions, but, for the most part, you can choose which type of music to work with."

A small victory. No more composing sonatas for seventy different orchestra members. I can stick to what I do best: four-minute-long songs that chronicle the epic disaster known as my love life.

"At the end of the year, you'll need to submit a senior thesis project to graduate. Since many of you are applying to music colleges, most of you will be able to use your thesis for your prescreening, or what you are doing for your audition for your thesis. I guess it depends on how on top of things you are.

"So here's the deal: Those of you wanting to do vocal compositions, you'll need to do a CD of original songs or a musical act that lasts at least forty minutes. Short form, three different sonatas or minuets for a total time of at least thirty minutes. And the orchestra folks, rescore a portion of a movie or television show. Again, at least thirty minutes." He starts handing out a sheet of paper with the requirements.

The CD is perfect; we've already been working on recording a few songs to sell some CDs at our shows. Plus, both Emme and I need recorded songs for our pre-audition for Juilliard. They require a pre-audition to see if you are even good enough for an audition. Fortunately, the other places we're applying to just have an audition.

I say that like we are purposely applying to the same schools.

We are not.

Well, at least she isn't. I'll admit to looking at her list before deciding where I was going to apply.

Until recently, Emme has been my biggest rock. But the rock turned into an avalanche a few weeks ago and now I don't know what she's thinking.

"Which brings us to the unpleasant matter of us giving out our charity to the rest of the school. That's right, school musical time."

Everybody in the room lets his or her disgust be known. We're required to perform in the orchestra of at least one all-school musical. It's a requirement of the other music programs — brass, percussion, piano, etc. — so it was deemed fairest to make the composition students do it as well.

"The first musical, *A Little Night Music*, is at the end of October and we need —"

Before he can even get the words out, both Emme and I shoot our hands up to volunteer at the exact same moment. She looks at me and laughs.

Mr. North shakes his head. "Why am I not surprised?"

Both Emme and I agree that it's best to get that prerequisite out of the way.

"Well, the good news is that they need two people: percussion and bass."

Emme leans in. "I'll flip you for percussion."

I shake my head. "You take it." She claps her hands together. Percussion will be the far less demanding of the two. The "real" percussion students will be assigned the drum kit and major roles. Emme will just need to fill in on a triangle or timpani if a song calls for it.

At this point, I'll do anything to make it so she never looks at me the way she did during the summer.

Lunch starts off eerily quiet, since Jack mercifully already did his usual pseudo-documentary account of our fates. Plus, we're all looking over our senior thesis requirements.

Jack throws the piece of paper on the table with purpose. "I know this may surprise you all, but I'm going to start working on this right away."

Ben laughs.

"Seriously. This is exactly what I need for CalArts, combining original composition with a movie. Genius."

Emme looks down at the table. She gets sad every time she's reminded that Jack wants to go across the country to school. Ben's first choice is Oberlin in Ohio. I'm the only person who's planning on staying on the East Coast, either at Juilliard, Berklee, Boston Conservatory, or the Manhattan School of Music. Although I did apply to the San Francisco Conservatory . . . because Emme has it on her list.

But we both want Juilliard. I think anybody who grows up in New York City with a passion for music wants to go there. You'd be crazy not to.

"Aww, come on, Red." Jack nudges Emme's shoulder playfully. "You've got the whole year to feast your eyes on all of this." He gestures over his body and raises his eyebrows at her.

She smiles reluctantly at him. Jack gets up and hugs Emme.

"I swear you're like a little lost puppy, Red. Damn you and those big green eyes. They get me every time."

Something catches Emme's attention and she quickly excuses herself from the table. My gaze follows her across the room as she approaches Carter and gives him a little hug.

Seriously, when did they become friends? We talk every day and she hasn't mentioned anything to me about him. I thought she told me everything, but I guess not.

Emme brings Carter over to the table. "Carter's going to join us for lunch," she announces. We make room for him. We've never had an outsider at our table before. I don't think I like this at all. We've had to share Emme with Sophie all this time, and now we've got to fight off the Soap Stud.

"Hey, guys, you were amazing today." He sits down and smiles at us. "Seriously, everybody in Drama was foaming at the mouth at having to compete with you guys for the Senior Showcase. You're totally the front-runners."

"Thanks, man." Jack shakes Carter's hand.

"Yeah, that's so nice of you." Ben tilts his head at Carter slightly.

"And I know you're upset" — Emme rubs her hand on Carter's back — "but you had one of the most difficult monologues to do, and I think you recovered nicely."

What the hell is going on? They are practically falling all over this no-talent hack. Fine, I'll give it to Emme and Ben that he's good-looking in that overly coifed all-American kind of way, but I expected more from Jack. Considering that Jack wants to be a composer for the big screen, I guess he sees Carter as his ticket into the business or whatever.

I mean, okay, I liked the first two *Kavalier Kids* movies as a kid, but seriously . . .

This is so not how I pictured senior year starting off. Granted, I didn't suddenly expect to mature completely, but how can I possibly work on my self-confidence when I've got Mr. Six-Pack sitting across from me? Especially when the three people most important to me are clearly enamored of this *Former Child Star*?

I don't say anything for the rest of lunch. Not when Carter breaks out a container full of chicken breast that serves as his entire meal. Not when I notice him looking at my cheeseburger and fries in envy. (At least I've got something over him; I got this "body" by stuffing my face with junk food, so he can just suck on that.) Not when Emme fills him in on our senior thesis. And especially not when Jack invites him to our rehearsal this weekend *at my apartment*.

I don't say a word.

And nobody seems to notice. Or care.

I'm ready to put this miserable day behind me when Emme approaches me with a smile on her face.

I smile back at her until she says, "Don't hate me." She pulls out The Calendar. I see Jack walking over, but as soon as he sees the all-too-familiar binder, he heads for the door.

"Jack's walking away." I rat him out.

Emme sprints to grab Jack, and he gives me the look of death as she drags him over.

"Come on, guys," she says, "this semester is going to be extremely complicated with college auditions, the senior thesis, and the showcase. We've got to figure everything out."

She opens up the color-coded weekly calendar that contains her academic assignments, her practice pieces, the band's schedule, and all the deadlines to pretty much everything on earth. She refuses to put it on her phone. She also writes out all her music. Pretty much everybody in class uses computers to record or write songs. But Emme uses good old paper and pencil.

It's so old-school. It's also utterly endearing.

I love that she still does it, especially after us picking on her about it since freshman year. I'd hate for her to change that or anything else about her. Except for her opinion about me — *that* I'd love to change.

She starts quizzing us on our schedules, assignments, and projects so she can figure out a practice schedule for the band.

I may be the front man, Jack may be the charisma, Ben may be the soul, but Emme is the heart of the band.

I think back to the time when I realized how much we needed her. How much *I* needed her. It was the first official fight of the band. And, of course, I was the reason for it.

Besides being the front man, I'm the pain in the ass of the band.

Our first few performances freshman year went okay. The sound was fine — only I was having some problems being the proper "leader" of the band. I thought I was walking into a rehearsal, but I was mistaken.

I could immediately tell by the silence that greeted me when I entered the room that something was wrong.

"We've got to talk." Jack gestured to the seat next to him.

I stayed standing.

Jack didn't seem surprised. "Okay, so no offense."

Generally speaking, when somebody starts a sentence with "no offense," what follows is something that you will take offense at.

"I mean, you know we all love you," Jack continued, only further delaying this awkward intervention.

I studied Ben to see if I could get a hint of what was going on, but he was just giving me a slight smile. I could tell he was smiling so the guilt wouldn't completely ooze off his face. Emme was worse. She was looking down at the ground; she wouldn't even look at me. She seemed even more uncomfortable than I was. And I had thought that was humanly impossible.

"Can you just get it over with?" I said with an even tone.

Jack continued to be the spokesperson of the group. "Look, you're an amazing musician and songwriter; I mean, it kills me that you're so talented." Now I was the one looking down at the floor. "Thank God I have the looks, because that just wouldn't be fair." Once again, Jack tried to lighten the mood. "It's just that . . . when you're onstage, you look miserable. You don't move around, you don't engage the audience, you just close your eyes and sing. We need you to be more of a . . . front man."

"Why do I have to be the front man?"

Jack threw his hands up. "Ah, because you're the lead singer."

"But that doesn't mean I have to be the one to always speak?"

Jack looked at Ben and Emme. "Yeah, it does."

"There are plenty of examples of bands that —"

Jack wouldn't even let me finish. "We don't really need a lesson on Rock Groups 101. It makes the most sense and, to be honest, you never freeze up like that when we rehearse."

"Have you ever thought that maybe it is a little intimidating to have to talk in front of a crowd? How would you like to have all that attention on you?"

"I'd love it."

"Then *you* do it."

"I can't really warm up the crowd when I'm behind my kit."

My stomach started to churn. I loved playing, I loved the band, but when I was onstage, I felt self-conscious. All eyes were on me while I sang. I felt this undeniable weight on my shoulders . . . and a little stupid.

"Emme should be the lead singer."

Emme finally looked up at me. The expression on her face reminded me of one of those girls in a slasher flick who's about to be stabbed by a serial killer. "I can't sing," she protested.

"You *can* sing," I argued. "You just choose not to." She lowered her head again.

Jack came over and put his hand on my shoulder. "Look, you're the best singer in the group. If you maybe opened your eyes every once in a while, you'd see that the girls in the audience like what they're hearing. Don't even pretend that you haven't noticed that you've gotten more attention since you first sang in the Freshman Focus Showcase. Tell him, Red."

Emme's mouth dropped open. "Why would I know if girls have been talking to Ethan? And, um, aren't we getting a little off track here?"

Thinking back to right after the showcase, I realized I *had* gotten more attention from girls. Kelsey had become really jealous, but I'd assumed it was from meeting Emme. She never liked the fact that there was a girl in our band, especially after she saw what Emme looked like.

Now there was an uncomfortable silence. I knew everybody was waiting for me to say something, but I couldn't see how I was supposed to magically become this outgoing person onstage. I didn't even feel comfortable talking in class, so I was sure the attention I received after the concert was from people who'd thought I was mute.

Jack was glaring at Emme, motioning for her to say something. She let out a deep sigh and stood up.

Her face matched the color of her hair. She closed her eyes and nodded to herself, her lips moving slightly. I tried to not smile; I knew exactly what was going on in her mind. I'd seen her do it a hundred times all semester. Usually she was trying to come up with a new lyric, but I wasn't sure what was about to come out of her mouth would be music to my ears.

She opened her eyes and approached me. She looked back at Jack and then crouched down so we were at eye level. "Ethan," she whispered so nobody else could hear, "did I ever tell you what I thought when I first heard you sing?" She didn't pause, as we both knew the answer to that. "I felt like

I heard you for the first time. That your singing voice is your true voice. I was blown away with how strong and warm it is, like I was being wrapped up in a cozy blanket. I could never do what you do, and I don't know how Sophie does it, either. But the thing is, I get the same feeling when I'm onstage with you that I do when I'm onstage with her. I don't get as nervous, because we're in it together and everything will turn out okay."

She got up and sat back down. Her eyes went back to the floor.

"Okay," I conceded. "I understand what you're all saying. I do, and all I can really say is that I'll work on it."

"That's what I'm talking about!" Jack patted me on the back. "We're in a band, which is supposed to be fun. Plus, it's a great way to meet hot chicks." He shot a look at Emme. "No offense."

Emme sighed and shook her head. "You know, I can always join an all-female group if I'm cramping your style."

"Aw, come on." Jack wrapped his arms around her. "I'm just teasing. You know we'd be nothing without you, right, Red?"

"Yeah, yeah," she said as she pushed him away.

While I wasn't extremely confident that I'd be able to rise to the occasion onstage, there was one thing that I was one hundred percent sure of:

I would be nothing without Emme.

"Ethan?" I look up to see Emme now, blue highlighter (my color) in her hand.

Jack shakes me. "Wake up, man. It isn't *that* painful. Now that I've done my time, I'm out of here. I'll see you guys later!" Jack leaves me alone with Emme.

We haven't really been alone lately. Not since . . .

I can tell she realizes it, too, because she gives me a small smile and puts her arm on my elbow. "Everything okay?"

I nod. I don't think what I'm currently going through would be described as being "okay," but I don't know what to say or do around her anymore. I've always been a useless dork around girls. Emme was the first girl who I never really felt self-conscious around. She was the first person to talk to me at school. She's one of my best friends. Actually, she is my best friend.

Yet here I am, standing across from the one person who probably despises me more than anybody. And, believe me, that list is pretty long.

"Listen," she says softly, giving a quick look around the hallway. "I don't want you to think . . . I'm really sorry if I . . ."

I shake my head. "No, it needed to be said."

She bites the corner of her lip. Then she opens her mouth slightly and I pray that whatever comes out of her mouth will make me feel better about myself, will silence the voices that have been screaming at me since that day. "Ethan . . ."

"EMME!" Sophie's voice blasts through the quiet, and like that, the moment is gone.

She runs over and hugs Emme. I ache when I see how happy this makes Emme. How she can't see what everybody else sees. That Sophie is just using her.

"How was your first day, Em?" She puts her arm around Emme and doesn't even bother to acknowledge my existence.

I'm wounded by her neglect.

"Carter told me that you're going to be in the band for *A Little Night Music*?"

And here we go.

Emme nods. "Yeah, both me and Ethan."

"Really?" Sophie looks over at me and forces out a smile. "That's so great! I'm thinking of auditioning for Desirée."

Wow, Sophie wants to play the part of a self-absorbed actress? That'll be a stretch.

"You totally should!" Emme encourages her. Emme always encourages her (or enables her, depending on who you're asking).

"Really?" Sophie acts surprised. "Do you think you'd help me get ready for the audition?"

Emme looks so happy. "Of course!"

I excuse myself. I've watched this play out for so long. Sophie needs Emme. Emme drops everything for Sophie.

I've never understood it. But Emme always stands up for Sophie. She's her best friend after all. (That always stings a little, since I'm the one who has to wipe her tears away whenever Sophie blows her off.)

But Sophie is the reason Emme is at CPA. And as much as it pains me, I will always be grateful to Sophie Jenkins for that one thing.

I'll be the first to admit that I'm a worrier and that I spend too much time stressing out over stupid things. And that I don't speak up when I should. But out of all the things that weigh me down on a daily basis, there is one item that I feel the need to finally get off my chest.

I've been working up the courage to do it all day. But I forgot about one thing.

Mr. Abs.

Carter's been watching us rehearse a few new numbers in the recording studio my parents built for me at the Park Avenue apartment (a benefit of being an only child).

He's a little too enthusiastic after every song. He can't seem to find another word to use besides *awesome*.

But everybody in the band is eating it up. Emme keeps smiling at him, Ben is practically throwing himself at him, and Jack is "totally stoked" to have him here.

I've decided that I'm finally going to tell Emme how I feel tonight. But I can't do it with Carter permanently attached to Emme like a barnacle.

She starts to wrap her guitar cord around her arms as we pack up for the night. I quickly move toward her as Ben asks Carter about some homework assignment.

"Hey, Emme, can you stay after so I can talk to you?"

Her eyes dart to Carter for a moment. "Um, sure." It comes out like a question. "I, ah, was going to . . ." She stops herself. "Yes, of course."

I think she knows this conversation has been a long time coming, and it's best if we both get it out of the way.

She goes over to talk to Carter, and Ben enthusiastically offers to leave with him. Jack keeps looking back between the two of us with a smile on his face. He's had this fantasy since the beginning that Emme and I would end up together.

But we all know Emme's thoughts on me as a boyfriend, so that is never going to happen.

"What's up?" She looks nervous. She keeps plucking at the guitar in her lap.

"What's going on with the Soap Stud?"

Emme glares at me.

I continue. "What? He comes to one gig and all of a sudden the two of you are . . . ?"

She gets up. "*This* is what you wanted to talk to me about? Do I even need to remind you who he's dating? Please, Ethan, you should know better. Just because a guy and a girl are friends doesn't mean there is anything romantic going on."

That's not devastating to hear. "No, that's not what I wanted to talk to you about, although I'm just trying to figure out when good ol' Six-Pack became such an important part of your life."

"He has a name." She reaches for her jacket.

"Okay. Carter." I take her jacket from her. "I'm sorry, I didn't mean to upset you. It's just . . ."

"I know. It's . . ." She bites her lip and my heart sinks. "I don't know." She falls back down on the couch, looking defeated. "The last few weeks have been weird. Sophie keeps disappearing, and I don't think I need to tell you how things have been between you and me. It's nice to have someone to talk to."

A lump rises in my throat. I used to be that person, but I don't know what I am to her anymore.

We sit in silence for a few moments. I figure she needs to hear it. "Do you have any idea how much you hurt me?" I try with every ounce of strength I have to not cry. But I think back to that day and what happened.

I walked into practice fifteen minutes late and I felt like crap.

"Sorry I'm late," I said. So it's not like I didn't say I was sorry.

"Dude, did you just wake up in a gutter?" Jack asked.

I knew I was a wreck. I hadn't slept in days, my hair was a mess, I hadn't shaved, my clothes were wrinkled and dirty.

"No," I told them. "Kelsey and I broke up."

Nobody said anything.

"For real this time. I screwed up. What a shock, Ethan screwed up. I told her everything that happened after last week's gig. About that girl. Whose name I can't even remember. I'm devastated. I threw away everything for someone whose name I don't even remember. I shouldn't have had those drinks before the gig. I just needed to get some courage. It was our biggest gig ever, you know?"

More silence.

"What? Am I missing something?"

They all exchanged glances. Ben finally was the one to speak. "Well, I mean, it isn't the first time you guys have broken up. Or the first time you cheated . . ."

Jack broke in. "Yeah, like every song you write is about it."

"But we're really done this time. There's no way she's going to take me back."

Ben sighed. "Doesn't she always?"

Emme let out a laugh. "Yeah, but she shouldn't."

"Oh! Burn!" Jack went to put his hand up to give Emme a high five, but she shrugged instead.

"I'm sorry, is this funny?" I couldn't believe that, out of everyone, Emme would take Kelsey's side in this.

"No, not at all." Emme rubbed her eyes. "It's not funny. It's exhausting, Ethan. We go through this all the time. So just write your forgiveness song so we can move on."

"Like it's that simple? Emme, really? How can you be so cold to me?"

Emme's face got flushed. "Get over yourself, Ethan."

"What?"

She got up. "How can I be so cold? Am I the one who continually cheats on my girlfriend? *That's* cold."

I stared at her. I'd never heard her say anything negative about anybody. Ever. Did she really think that about me?

"You know what gets me? You really are an amazing person, seriously. I used to respect you so much."

The words *used to* stung.

"You're one of my closest friends, but when I think about the stuff you do . . . sometimes I don't know why I trust you so much. I've never met anybody who hurts someone as much as you do. And now you've started drinking and doing God knows what before our shows. You've become so unpredictable onstage, we never know what you're going to do."

This riled me up. "Okay, so first I'm too quiet, now I'm too unpredictable. Can I ever do anything right?"

"Don't blame your behavior on us. Take responsibility for once."

"This isn't easy for me, you know."

Emme got in my face. "I'll make it easy for you. STOP CHEATING."

We were all surprised by Emme screaming. Jack, who is always smiling, looked stunned.

"Just STOP IT. Oh, you don't know how you can get her back? STOP CHEATING, Ethan! It's not that hard. Really, it isn't. Or, better yet, stop getting back together and making promises you can't keep."

I tried to defend myself, but came up blank.

"You want to know what I think?" Emme asked.

Normally, the answer would have been yes, but not at that moment.

"You do this to yourself, put your finger repeatedly on the self-destruct button because you need it to write. It would be fine if you weren't bringing others down with you. Have you for once thought about how it must feel for Kelsey? All you do is think about yourself, what a mess you're in. Your pain. But what about Kelsey? The one YOU cheat on? She probably agonizes every time she can't come to one of our shows, because of what happens when she doesn't come. You CHEAT. You take whatever girl comes along and pays you a compliment and you forget about Kelsey.

"But lately that hasn't been enough, has it? You need more things to feel sorry for yourself about, so you go get drunk. It's like you're afraid of being alone or coherent so you can deal with whatever is the real problem you have. And I feel sorry for you about that. But only for that. For the rest of the stuff, I'm just sick of it.

"We all are. So just figure it out, because I can't do this anymore if you're going to continue to be like this."

I looked around to see Jack and Ben nodding.

"Honestly, Ethan, I don't know who you are anymore. But whoever this is, I don't like him very much."

I didn't know how to react or what to say. I still don't. All I do know is that it has been weeks and it's still awkward. We both stare at each other. Once again, there's tension between us.

"You really did hurt me," I say. "But I needed to hear it. You were right, and I think I've been better. Or at least I've tried to be."

She nods.

"I'm not falling into my old traps. I'm not making any promises I can't keep. I'm not drinking or doing anything that affects the band on or off the stage in a negative way."

She keeps nodding.

"You said what you had to say because you care about me. So that's what I'm doing now. Sort of returning the favor."

Emme looks up at me for the first time. "What does any of this have to do with Carter?"

"It doesn't. It has to do with the senior project."

"Oh." I don't know what she thought I was going to say, but that certainly wasn't it.

"I guess it's pretty obvious that we'll be working on our projects together." She nods in agreement. "And I'm more than happy to have you record your songs here, but I have one condition."

She looks at me quizzically.

"You have to sing your songs."

She gets up. "Ethan, you know I can't sing."

"No, I don't know that. Because you *can* sing. You don't seem to realize that, because someone's been brainwashing you all these years into thinking that she's the superior singer."

She clenches her jaw. "You've made your thoughts on Sophie abundantly clear. But she *is* the better singer."

"Your songs would be a million times better if you sang them. Those songs are *your* heart and soul. You're lending them to somebody who could never have as much heart as you have, even if she tried."

"I can't —"

I cut her off. "You've got to step up, Emme. You've got to let people hear your voice, hear *you*. You're better than being stuck in the background."

I take her hands.

"You're my best friend. You're the most remarkable person in my life. And . . . I want you to believe in yourself as much as I do. I told you that I'm not making any promises that I can't keep. So here's a promise to you. I will be there with you every step of the way and do whatever I can to help."

I reach up and wipe away the tear that has begun to work its way down her cheek.

"I don't think I can do it," she says quietly.

"Yes, you can."

I kiss her lightly on her forehead and wrap my arms around her.

I know she's scared. Singing in front of an audience is intimidating. But if I can do it, she can.

I did it for her. Pretty much everything I've done out of my comfort zone, I've done for Emme.

The voices in my head quiet significantly as I sit there with her.

There is only one voice left.

There is only one thing left to say to her. But I've used up all my courage.

So as I hold her, I think in my head: *Emme Connelly, I love you. And I've been in love with you since the first day we met.*

SOPHIE

*O*kay, so not everything has gone according to my Plan. It's my senior year, my last chance to make a statement at this school. To stand out. To be a star.

So, no, my Plan hasn't worked out. But there is no Plan B.

I don't know where it all went wrong. At this point, I was supposed to be the biggest star in the school. The one that the entire incoming freshman class would follow around and aspire to be.

But no, I'm stuck in some cruel otherworld where the tables have turned and I'm the one forced to practically beg Emme for help. And the cruel irony of it all is that *I'M* the person who had to basically drag her here kicking and screaming. And what does she do to repay me? She goes off and becomes part of a band that everybody here seems to love.

The least she could do at this point is help me get the part in *A Little Night Music*.

"Are you sure I can't help?" Amanda offers. "I can practice the songs with you."

I turn my back to her as I examine my closet. "You're so sweet, Mandy. It's just that Emme's in the band and will be playing during the auditions, so she's got the inside edge that I need to nail the part."

I start to rummage through my closet for the perfect audition outfit. I'm so sick of all my clothes. For whatever reason, Carter doesn't want to go to any openings or premieres lately, so I haven't had an excuse to beg my parents for money for a new outfit.

I'm so sick of begging people for help. Just wait until I'm out of CPA and become a star. They'll all come groveling to *me* to thank them when I win my Best New Artist Grammy.

"You'll totally get the part, Soph. You're the most amazing singer in the entire school. Sarah Moffitt —"

I turn around quickly and snap at Amanda, "I thought we'd agreed to not mention that name."

Amanda shuts her big mouth.

Sarah Moffitt. For whatever reason, she's been every teacher's favorite student since day one. It's like some Big Conspiracy Against Sophie. She's given all the lead parts. She's not even that good a singer. Sure, she has better range than I do. So what? She has, like, zero stage presence.

I made sure she was auditioning for a different role before I signed up for Desirée. (Of course she's chosen Madame Armfeldt — if she wants to play my mother, an old hag, that's fine by me.) She's been handed every role we've competed against. What ticked me off the most was last year, she got to play Rizzo in *Grease* while I had to be Frenchy. I didn't get any solos to sing. It was annoying. But now we're seniors and have to fight over the lead parts. I chose Desirée because of the song "Send in the Clowns." It will be my moment to shine. Every teacher who has placed me as "average" — a word that I do not identify with and never have — will see that I belong in the Senior Showcase.

That's the only focus I have this year. That showcase. I will get a spot, no matter what I have to do. And when those talent scouts see me, game over. I'll have a record deal before we graduate. That's all I've ever wanted. And I will do whatever it takes to get it.

I pull out a fitted skirt and blazer. "I figure I'll put my hair up like this" — I pull my shiny dark brunette hair in a twist — "wear a simple, yet flattering suit, pearl earrings . . . a classic, elegant look. A little unexpected as well. I'm sure everybody else will have normal school clothes on. I should probably . . ."

I pick up the phone to call Emme. "Hey, Emme!"

Amanda sulks on the couch. She desperately wants to be the one to write my songs for me. But she can't. Emme is a way better songwriter.

"Hi, Sophie!"

No matter how long I go without talking to Emme, she's always there for me. She's a true friend.

"I have a question about the auditions. Do you know if they're expecting anybody to arrive in period costume?"

"Um, the show is set at the beginning of the nineteenth century, so I doubt it."

"No, I know, but I figure I should try to look conservative. Do you know what the sight song is?"

For the audition, we have to sing a song from the musical — I'll obviously be doing "Send in the Clowns" — but then we're also forced to sing a song from sheet music, completely unprepared. Which I've always hated to do. Plus, it makes zero sense because all the songs we're performing are from the musical. There aren't any originals. I think Dr. Ryan, the director of the musical, is doing it solely to make it difficult for me to get the part. She beyond favors Sarah, it's so ridiculous. I swear, I even once heard Sarah call Dr. Ryan by her first name, Pam. Like *that* is appropriate student-teacher behavior. It seems that Sarah is doing whatever it takes to get ahead, so I'm just following her lead.

"You know that I'm not allowed to tell you that," Emme says softly.

I wish Emme realized that all is not fair in auditions and war.

"I know, but I get so nervous during auditions, especially if you aren't there backing me up."

"But I will be there."

Dammit. "Yeah, but it won't be just you and me. I feel all alone in this, and you know, I . . ." I know what will work with

Emme. I start working up tears. "I really need this, Em. And you are the only one who can help me. I need you. *Please.*"

I sniffle while Emme takes her time to respond. Amanda flips through one of my magazines.

"The problem is that it's an original song. Dr. Ryan asked Ethan to use one of his songs for the audition."

Crap. Ethan. Probably the person who would most love to see me fail. That guy has not liked me since day one and he's all overprotective of Emme, like she belongs to him. She owes him nothing. *I'm* the reason she's at CPA, not him.

"Why does he hate me so much, Em? Why?" I wish Dr. Ryan could see me now; I'd be guaranteed the part. My voice cracks and everything.

"He doesn't . . . oh, Sophie. I'm so sorry that you're upset. Let me see what I can do."

"You know that I'm eternally grateful to you, right, Em? I'm going to entitle my first album *Emme is my BFF and I owe her everything.*"

I go on and on about how amazing and wonderful she is and pretend that talking to her has made everything better. I hang up the phone and see Amanda staring at me. "Oh, Emme!" She exaggerates her words. "You are the best thing ever, thank you for getting off your high horse for two seconds to help li'l ol' me."

I bust out laughing. I can't believe how needy I sounded.

"Enough about Emme." I pick up my outfit to try it on. "I've got a role to win."

★ ★ ★ ★ ★ ★ ★ ★ ★ ★ ★ ★ ★ ★

Sometimes it's like pulling teeth with Emme. You'd think she'd want to help her best friend land a role that could change her life, but she keeps saying things like she'll "get in trouble" or Ethan will "kill" her.

Does she not realize that this is how show business works? It's a tough place and you have to take whatever advantages you can. For me, that's knowing as much about the audition as possible. And the person who can give me that is Emme.

Although, if I have to keep forcing tears with her, I'm going to have nothing left for the actual audition. Not with the constant role I play in *Who Loves Emme More*? I've even been wearing the bracelet she bought me for Christmas or my birthday or something a few years ago. I know how much it means to her that I wear it. It's not really my style, it's cutesy — like Emme. My style is more fashion-forward, modern chic.

Anyway, I decide to sit it out. She'll crack if I give her the silent treatment.

She just sits there and studies on her bed. She isn't even looking at me. Or noticing that I'm mad at her.

Different strategy. "Ahem!" I say loudly.

She looks up. Bingo.

"So sorry, Em. I'm just thinking about the Senior Showcase and hoping that I have enough major parts coming up to be considered for the audition."

We aren't even allowed to audition for the showcase; we are asked. And even then, your spot isn't guaranteed.

"But it won't matter, I guess. I'm singing one of your songs after all. No one can say no to an Emme Connelly song."

Flattery, my dears, gets you everywhere.

She smiles at me . . . then starts reading from her history book.

"Have you decided what songs you're going to put on your CD for your senior thesis?"

She looks up. "Um, not really. I know a few. I'm starting to work on a new song for the showcase, plus I need a couple more for the college auditions."

Then something hits me.

"You know what's awesome. Your senior project is perfect. It helps you with your college applications and we can use it as my demo."

Emme bites her lip. Her and her stupid lip biting. Just flippin' spit it out if you have something to say!

"Is there a problem?" I try to say sweetly.

She shakes her head. "No, it's just that I didn't think you were going to sing on it. You haven't . . ."

I know we didn't talk about it, but I just assumed. Plus . . .

"Well, if I don't sing on it, who will?" Does she not realize I've been doing her a favor all these years? Giving my voice to her songs.

"I am." She says it so softly.

Obviously this is some sick joke she's playing.

I give a light laugh. "Oh, Emme, you almost had me. You know that I'd be more than happy to help you out. Plus, when I send out my demos, it will put your songs out there as well. It's what friends do."

I can't believe Emme would forget that she's always been a huge part of my Plan. Yes, my demo will get me recognition with managers and labels, but this is how she'll get her break as a songwriter and producer as well. It's how the business works. I've done my research, so a little appreciation would be nice.

Emme shakes her head. "I know, but it's just . . . we're recording in Ethan's studio and it's sort of a condition of his. . . ."

"Oh. I get it. His condition is to ruin my life. Is that it? First, he refuses to let me see the song for the audition tomorrow and now he wants to prevent me from getting a record contract?"

Emme looks upset, like she's about to cry. I don't see what she has to cry about. It isn't her life that's being sabotaged, it's mine.

"Sophie, he thinks it would be good for the college recruiters to hear me sing it, that's all. We can record your vocals as well and do a demo for you."

Well, that's better. But there's still something she's not giving me.

"I'm sorry, Em. I know you'd never betray me. I'm just so worked up about tomorrow's audition. If I just had some idea of the other song, just a little, teeny, tiny clue, I'd feel so much better."

Oh, what a surprise, she's biting her lip. She walks over to the full-size keyboard in her room.

"Okay. I don't know it that well since I'm not playing on it. I'm just going to sit here and play what I remember. This is between you and me."

I get up to give her a hug. "Oh, Emme! You have no idea how much I appreciate this. You're the best!"

I sit back down on her bed and close my eyes and she starts playing a melody. I begin to hum along to it and play it in my head for the rest of the night.

I totally nail the audition. I know my "Send in the Clowns" is killer, but when Dr. Ryan hands me the sheet music for the sight-reading portion, I bite my lip (in honor of Emme!) and pretend to study it. I sing the first half of the song exactly as written, but then, for the last verse, I close my eyes and put my Sophie touch on it.

When I open my eyes, Dr. Ryan clearly looks impressed. Ethan looks pissed. Like I care.

"How'd it go?" Carter greets me at my locker.

"Incredible!"

He gives me a hug. "That's great!"

"Listen, I've got my bag to get ready for tonight, so I figured we can go to your place so I can change."

Carter and I are going to some art opening tonight. Totally not my thing, but it's the first social thing he's been up for in a while. I got this black cocktail dress and funky red shoes to go with the SoHo crowd. At least, I hope it's in SoHo, or at the Met or MoMA. Somewhere with fabulously trendy people and an awesome swag bag.

"I thought we'd just have dinner down the street, since the exhibit is here."

"What?"

Carter shakes his head. "I told you it was Trevor's exhibit of his impressionist era–influenced paintings."

I'm sure he did, but I have no idea what any of that really means. "I didn't realize it was a CPA thing, plus I don't know who Trevor is."

"Trevor Parsons. He's only the best art student in school."

He says this like being the best art student is a big thing in this school. The stage is what matters.

"I thought we were going to some fabulous opening. We haven't done that in forever. Can't you call Sheila Marie and see if there's anything going on tonight that's *fun*?"

"But I want to go to this. And we can't call Sheila Marie. She's no longer my publicist. I don't really want to deal with the press anymore."

Here I had the most amazing audition, and Carter has to ruin it by taking me to some lame school event and firing his publicist.

It used to be fun to be with Carter, doing things like going to openings and getting my picture taken. But lately he's been so weird. He doesn't like to go out, he's been talking about Emme just a little too much (it's always about her, isn't it?), and he's even cutting down on his hours on the soap opera. If I wanted to date a normal high school boy, I'd go out with some guy back in Brooklyn who'd be dying to be seen with me on his arm.

"I'm sorry, I thought you knew." Carter puts his muscular arm around me.

I lean into him. Carter's a good guy and sometimes I can't believe he's my boyfriend. I dream big, but he's so much more than I thought I would get. It's not just his looks or his fame (although those help). I'm just thankful he isn't that emotional a person; I've got too many of those people in my life as is. Plus, we look really good together. I figure once I get my record contract, he'll come to some of my gigs, get me some press attention (mental note: talk to his mom about hiring a new publicist ASAP), then we'll break up right before my album release, which the tabloids would love: "Single Sophie Stays Strong."

I can practically see the cover now.

So I'll go to some stupid art opening. It's the least I can do.

After all, today has otherwise been a very, very good day.

You'd think that a school based on the study of performance and art would have better lighting.

After we eat and I change back into my normal school clothes for the day (thankfully, I wore a very cute fitted navy dress, just in case I didn't have time to change into my outfit for the audition), Carter and I walk into the large art studio that's hosting the exhibit. It's mostly filled with the art students . . . and, of course, Emme and her entourage: Ethan, Ben, Jack, and Chloe. At least I know someone here.

Emme comes up to us, with Ethan following obediently behind her. "Hey, guys!" She gives us both hugs while Ethan just stands there.

"Sophie, you were wonderful at the audition today." Emme is beaming.

Ethan decides to ruin this nice moment by speaking. "Yes, it's remarkable how well you were able to pick up on my song. It's almost like, I don't know, you'd heard it before."

Emme's eyes grow wide.

Carter looks between Ethan and me. "What's this?"

I wish Ethan didn't hate me so much. He really is one of the most talented songwriters in school. It would be nice to have him on my side. I know he could write some truly amazing songs for me.

I turn to Carter. "Part of the audition was sight-reading, which always makes me so nervous. I was sick to my stomach over it. But when I found out it was a song by Ethan, I got so excited because I've always wanted to sing one of his songs. And it was so beautiful, it practically sang itself. I don't think anybody could do a bad job singing it."

Ethan's reaction doesn't change. But Emme eats it up. "Exactly! You did such a good job and it *is* one of my favorite songs by Ethan. We're going to record it this weekend for his Juilliard pre-audition."

"Impressive." Carter's attention moves back to the group after he scans the paintings on the wall. "You have to pre-audition?"

"Yeah," Emme says, "you have to send in a tape, and that factors into whether or not you get asked to audition."

"Yikes!" Carter makes a face. It isn't very attractive.

"I know, and to add insult to injury, the Juilliard audition is two weeks after the showcase, so it will *not* be a fun winter. That is, if we get into the showcase and are asked to audition."

"Are you two auditioning together?" Carter gestures at Emme and Ethan.

Emme shakes her head. "No, we're playing on each other's audition tapes. But the band will be auditioning for the showcase . . . if we're asked."

"There's no way you guys aren't going to be in the showcase. No way."

I wish Carter showed that much enthusiasm about *me* being in the showcase.

Emme smiles at Carter. I don't know what's going on between the two of them, but I don't like it one bit. Emme has had a few dates, but the band keeps her too busy to have a serious boyfriend. Not that it isn't obvious to everybody that Ethan worships her. Well, obvious to everybody but Emme.

"Hey, Carter." Emme nudges him. "Let's go say hi to Trevor!" She grabs him by the elbow and leads him off.

Ethan just stares at me.

"What?"

"I know you pressured Emme into playing the song for you."

"I don't know what you're talking about."

"Yes, you do."

"I'll admit I asked her about it, but Emme plays by the rules too much to do something 'illegal' like give me an advantage." Emme's naïve belief in playing fair guarantees that she will not make it in the music business. If she thinks CPA is cutthroat, wait until she gets to the real world. No one, not even Ethan, can protect her then.

"No, she wouldn't do that . . . without being manipulated."

"Honestly, Ethan, think what you want. I'm telling you the truth."

He scowls at me. "Please. You are not that good an actress." He walks away and heads over to the rest of his groupies.

Let me think; I was able to get holier-than-thou Emme to basically cheat to give me the leg up, promise me that I can record a demo that I can send out, and get her to write a song for the Senior Showcase . . . because we are BFFs. Not to mention that I've got the most famous student at CPA as my boyfriend.

I think that makes me an excellent actress.

Opening night.

For the past six weeks I've been pulling eighteen-hour days: Wake up at six, exercise, eat, go to school, study for two hours, and then rehearse my role as Desirée in *A Little Night Music*.

My parents and Emme worry that skipping college and going right into the "grind" will be too much for me. But I've proven that I can not only handle long and grueling days, but thrive. This is what I want to do. I love the busy days, rehearsing, performing. I understand that being worn out is part of this business. I know exactly what it'll take to be a star. And I'm not afraid to go for it.

I step out on the stage and feel the warmth of the spotlight.

There is no question that this is where I belong. Every eyeball is on me.

Lead role in a major CPA production.

Check!

Now all I need is to land the lead spot in the showcase and it will all be mine.

EMME

*S*ophie is amazing. She gets a well-deserved standing ovation every night.

I look over to see her being congratulated at the after-party of our final performance. She's beaming, as she should be.

"Here you go." Ethan hands me some punch. "To getting it over with."

We clink our glasses together. With our musical requirement out of the way, we can concentrate on our final project.

"I'm sick to my stomach thinking about the fact that we mailed our applications."

Ethan and I went together to mail our pre-audition applications and CDs before tonight's show. I don't think I would've had the courage to do it if he hadn't been with me, practically pulling the envelope out of my hand.

"Your songs are incredible. You *sounded* incredible."

"Don't remind me." I have a hard time listening to me sing. The first take we did of my vocals was awful. But I got used to singing; it helped that Ethan was being so supportive. Although he is the only person I've allowed to hear me sing. Well, Ethan and the admissions staff at Juilliard. "What did you make me do?"

He laughs at me. "Oh, I don't know, help you accomplish your dreams. Really, a simple thank-you will suffice."

"Thank you." I raise my glass to him.

"Don't mention it. Actually, mention it . . . often."

I don't exactly know what's happened to him, but he's really turned around the last few weeks. There's no drama, no self-pity; he's just plain, regular Ethan.

"Okay, I have a favor to ask."

He looks at me with a smirk on his face. "Oh, really? This ought to be good."

"You have to promise me that you'll tell me the second you hear from Juilliard and the other schools." He scowls slightly. He's always the first one of us to get his CPA acceptance for the following semester, but he always waits to tell us until we all receive ours. "This is a really big deal, and I want you to feel like you can celebrate it and not worry about if I've heard anything. Promise."

He pauses for a second before he responds. "Okay."

"Say it."

"Promise." He looks down at the floor for a few beats before he looks up at me. And he seems nervous. "Emme, I need you to know that —"

"Hey, guys!" Tyler Stewart approaches us. "Great job!" Tyler was the lead pianist in the orchestra for the show. I also had a little bit of a crush on him when we were in Advanced Piano last year.

"Thanks, although I really didn't do much. *You* were extraordinary." I feel my cheeks grow hot.

He smiles at me. "Oh, come on, that triangle can be pretty tricky."

I laugh like an idiot. I've never been good at flirting. Ever. That's probably why I've only had about four dates at CPA. I like to blame it on how busy we are. But it's because I've got absolutely no skills when it comes to boys. Sure, I love the guys in the band, but they're like brothers to me. There was never any question that we were only going to be friends, so there's never been any pressure to be anybody but me.

"Well, I'm a girl of many talents."

Oh, my goodness. What did I just say?

Fortunately, Tyler laughs and replies, "I'm sure you are."

Ethan interrupts us. "I'm ready to head out."

"Oh, okay." Tyler looks disappointed.

The guys in the band are extremely protective of me, and always have been. There was this one guy who used to come to our gigs all the time last year and talk to me afterward. The guys referred to him as my stalker. He was innocent enough (and only fourteen), but Jack always stood over him like my bodyguard.

"Um, actually, I was going to hang around and go back to Brooklyn with Sophie," I say. That's technically not a lie. Sophie and I didn't make plans to go back together, but I just assumed. Plus, it lets me stay longer and talk to Tyler without me appearing desperate.

Tyler lights up. "Great!"

Ethan hesitates. "Okay, see you tomorrow." He gives me a quick hug and nods at Tyler.

After Ethan leaves, Tyler leans in. "I've got a confession to make. Ethan intimidates the crap out of me. That guy is a genius."

I nod. "He really is. I've watched him write songs, and it just comes out of him so fast. It's like it's completely effortless, and I, of course, have to spend days, weeks even, obsessing over the simplest chord progression." I think Ethan's probably bored with our assignments in class, he's always the first one to finish. He'd never admit it since the rest of us struggle, but I always wonder why he puts up with all the drama of CPA when he's one of the few students who doesn't really need the school's help. He's already a brilliant songwriter. "I have to admit that I was terrified the first time I had to play something I wrote in front of him. But he's also one of the most supportive people in the program."

Tyler puts his hand in his pockets. "Yeah, that's great . . . um, since we're confessing things, I also want to admit that I'm glad he left and that you're still here."

I think, *Play it cool, Emme.* But "Me, too!" bursts from my lips with a little too much excitement.

Tyler and I sit on a couch and talk for the rest of the time. I don't even notice when Sophie leaves. Or that Ethan texts me four times to see if I made it home okay. Or that Tyler and I are the last ones there.

All I know is that I have a date planned with Tyler Stewart.

Leave it to Jack to figure out something is going on.

"What aren't you telling me, Red? You've got this little mischievous smile on your face."

"I do not."

He puts his hands on my shoulders and leans in to stare into my eyes.

"Yes, you do. I'll admit, it suits you well. You should be a troublemaker more often."

The four of us sit down in composition class. The last thing I need is those three giving me grief for my date on Wednesday with Tyler.

Thankfully, Mr. North starts class, which is the only thing that can quiet Jack down (somewhat). But he keeps tugging on my hair as Mr. North fills us in on the next CPA concert.

"Okay, guys, the alumni concert is coming up. I don't need to remind you that some of our most prestigious alumni, and those with the deepest pockets, come each year to be wowed by the students. Now that you're seniors, you get the privilege of putting on the show. The theme this year is Icons. Each performance will need to feature an icon or an iconic piece from one of the decades since CPA was founded. A representative from each group needs to come up and pick a decade out of the hat."

Jack gets up for us and takes a piece of paper out of the hat. He unfolds it and nods his head with a big smile on his face. He shows Mr. North the paper and holds it out to us as he comes back to his seat. "The eighties."

The other four groups pick their decades, and Mr. North reminds us that this is the last all-school performance before the showcase audition invitations are handed out.

"Okay," Ethan starts us off. "We've got to make a statement here. I'm thinking that whatever we choose, it should be something loud, something big, very rock-heavy. Last year I wanted to fall asleep from all the power ballads. Just because some of the alumni are elderly, it doesn't mean that we can't spice things up."

We all agree. Plus, being loud always helps me with any nerves I have onstage. Churning out big power chords fast has a calming effect on me. I'm probably the only person who finds performing punk music therapeutic.

"Why don't we put a punk spin on whatever song we choose?" I say.

"That's what I'm talking about!" Jack agrees.

We throw out names of the eighties' musical icons: Madonna, Prince, Bruce Springsteen, The Police, and so on. Until we settle on the biggest of them all.

Michael Jackson.

Ben hits his hand against the table. "I've got it. 'Beat It.' It's got the sick guitar lick and solo. Ethan, I know you can take it to the next level. Plus, Jack can hash out an intense beat on the drum, and Emme and I will keep up just fine."

It's unanimous. I pull out The Calendar and start to figure out practice times.

"Man, I'm excited about this." Jack is already tapping out a beat with his fingers. "I want to start working on it ASAP. What's everybody's week like? If we get even a basic idea down, maybe we can do a rough version at our gig on Friday night?"

"I'm free," Ben offers.

"Me, too," Ethan says with his eyes closed. I know he's figuring out his part in his head.

"Yeah. Me, too, except for Wednesday."

All three of them look at me. "What's Wednesday?" Jack's got one eyebrow raised.

"I have plans."

Jack scoffs. "Plans? With who?"

"Am I not allowed to have plans that don't involve you guys?"

"No," they say in unison.

"Whatever."

Jack, never one to let things go, prods on. "Sophie? Carter?"

"No, I . . . Okay, I'll tell you, but please don't make a big deal about it."

Jack gasps. "Emme Connelly, do you have a date?"

"Oh, just forget it."

"We certainly will *not* forget it."

"Fine, I'm going to dinner with Tyler. Happy?"

Jack shakes his head. "Nicely done, Red."

I pull out The Calendar to write up our practice schedule until the concert in three weeks. Ben spends the rest of the class grilling me on my date, with Jack making disparaging comments. And Ethan keeps his eyes closed for the rest of the time.

At least one of them respects what little privacy I have.

Over the past three years, I've had to audition seven times to be a student at CPA, I've performed countless times as part of an assignment or with the band, and now I'm singing on an album that will serve as my senior thesis . . . not to mention part of my application to the top music school in the country.

However, I don't think anything has made me as nervous as walking into the bistro where I'm meeting Tyler.

He stands up from the table where he's waiting for me. His wavy brown hair is just slightly shorter than Ethan's and he's sporting just the right amount of stubble. He's got his normal outfit of dark jeans with a button-down shirt — this time it's white with thin black stripes.

He greets me with a kiss on the cheek and a hug.

"You look beautiful," he says.

I smile at him as I put my shaking hands in my lap. Sophie was busy, so Ben came over and helped me pick out my outfit: black leggings with a long, gray sweater, and black riding boots. He said I looked classic, yet contemporary.

We make small talk about class and music assignments. Tyler is applying to most of the same schools as Ethan and I.

"I submitted my application to Juilliard yesterday," he says as our pasta entrées arrive. "I thought I was going to throw up."

"Me, too," I confide. "I stood there in front of the mailbox for what seemed like an eternity. Ethan had to pry the envelope out of my hand."

"Oh." Tyler picks at his fettuccini. "I guess I should have assumed that he's applying as well. Not like he needs Juilliard. You know, I thought you guys were a couple for the longest time. He's always around you."

This isn't the first time that somebody thought this about us. But he's pretty shy when he's not onstage, so he only really talks to me and the other members of the band. Nobody ever seems to think he's with Ben, though. Which always irritates Ben. I smile as I think of Ben saying "What? Like I couldn't get you if I really tried?"

"What's so funny?" Tyler asks.

"Oh, just thinking of something. Anyway, Ethan's one of my closest friends. All the guys in the band are."

Tyler nods knowingly. "I wish I could say the same for the

rest of the piano section. But there's usually only a need for one pianist. Not a way to make good friends."

"I can only imagine."

Tyler lets out a laugh. "Yeah, it isn't pretty. Although I think the vocal department is worse. I accompany Sarah Moffitt a lot, so I've heard some interesting stories."

I nod since I've heard a lot of stories, many of them *about* Sarah, from Sophie. I realize every day how lucky I am to be in my department. Sure, we compete for songs against each other, but there's never been any sabotage . . . at least that I'm aware of.

"So what are you auditioning with?" I decide to change the subject away from the vocal department.

Tyler begins to enthusiastically go over his audition pieces. We don't discuss CPA for the rest of the meal.

As he walks me to the subway, he holds my hand. We walk slowly for several blocks, and as we approach the entrance, butterflies start swirling in my stomach.

"Are you going to be okay getting home?" He steps out of the way of pedestrians coming from an arriving train.

I nod my head. "Yes. Thanks for dinner."

He takes a step toward me and cups his hand around my chin. He leans in and kisses me gently. "Call me when you get home."

Since I've apparently become mute, I nod again.

I practically float through the turnstile and back to Brooklyn.

★　★　★　★　★　★　★　★　★　★　★　★　★　★

We decide to run through "Beat It" during our sound check on Friday night. We're the second of three acts performing at the Ravine, a new concert venue in the Village. It's the biggest place we've played, the stage is a lot bigger than we're used to . . . and higher up.

"No stage diving, Red," Jack says as he looks down at the five feet that separate the stage and the floor. We're used to being on a small riser.

Ethan keeps going over his guitar solo. His fingers are moving so fast, I don't think any of us will be able to keep up with him.

"You know," Ben says once Ethan stops, "I don't think we should play it tonight. It's not that I don't think we could do a good job or anything, but I'd rather keep what we're doing a surprise until the alumni concert."

"Good point," Jack agrees. "Best to floor everybody then." He rearranges the set list a few more times before it's done. Since there'll be more people here — most likely for the headlining band — we're starting off with a few covers to warm up the crowd before we do our original songs.

We head back to our dressing room. Everybody starts with their pre-concert rituals. Jack and Ben play video games and fake argue with each other. I do homework (I'm so hardcore!) and Ethan paces around.

A cheer erupts from Ben as Jack throws down his controller. "Oh, I didn't realize we could cheat," Jack says drily.

Ben gets up and does a small dance. "You're such a sore loser."

Jack crosses his arms and pulls his bottom lip out.

Ben turns his back on him. "Emme, Ethan, I'm going to check out the first band; you guys want to join?" He then looks over at Jack. "You are of course welcome, Sir Pouts-a-Lot."

Ben heads out of the dressing room, and the three of us follow him. As soon as we exit the room, we see Chloe approaching us with Carter . . . and Tyler.

"Where are you guys off to?" Chloe goes over to Jack and gives him a hug. His pout evaporates and he wraps his arms around her. Ah, young love. "We wanted to wish you good luck!"

Tyler comes up to me and gives me a quick kiss on the lips. "I brought these for you." Behind his back is a bouquet of roses.

"Thanks," I say quietly.

Jack starts to say something, but Chloe hits him. "Um, yeah, anyway . . ." Jack motions toward the side of the stage. "We were going to check out the City Kings, and um . . ." Jack can't stop looking between Tyler and me. I feel the entire group's eyes are on us and I don't know what to do.

I grab Carter's arm and lead him to the side of the stage, just as a group made of students from the LaGuardia school start their set.

"How are things?" I shout above the loud guitars blaring through the room.

He smiles at me. "Good. I'll be soap-free by spring!" Carter fills me in on his progress of moving away from acting. He's even looking into private art lessons.

"That's fantastic." A ballad starts playing and Tyler comes over, wrapping his arms around my waist. As if I wasn't nervous enough before facing a packed crowd of five hundred people.

We all stand there and watch the band. I can't really concentrate on the music — my entire focus is on Tyler's hands and his breath hitting my neck. Jack nudges me a few times playfully, but I try to stare out at the stage and look like I'm not freaking out inside.

The City Kings finish their set and we head to our dressing room.

"I've never seen a show from the side before," Chloe says. "That was cool."

Jack puts his arm around her. "You can see our shows from anywhere you want. I know I don't have a bad angle."

The stage manager pops his head in the door and yells "Five minutes!"

"Yikes, we better get going." Chloe gives Jack a quick kiss.

"Yeah, break a leg." Tyler gives me a quick kiss as well.

Before the door even closes, Jack starts in on me. "Ooh, Red! You've finally snagged a groupie. My little girl's all growns up!"

"Ah, guys," Ben interrupts us. "Do you know where Ethan is?"

I didn't even realize he wasn't there. It's not like the room is that big. "Where did he —"

Ben opens the door and looks down the hallway. "He left right when the band started — I thought he was going back here. Maybe he's just getting some fresh air or running around."

Ben and I head in opposite directions and I see Ethan talking to one of the members of the headlining band, Prophecy's Cupid, an honest-to-goodness signed band.

"Hey, we're on soon!" I call out.

Ethan turns his head toward me and I immediately smell alcohol on him. He hasn't had a drink before a show since The Incident. He used to have a drink to loosen up his nerves, and I guess none of us ever said anything to him because we knew how nervous he was about being the front man. But then he started to have a couple more drinks that led to more Ethan drama, including his subsequent meltdown over Kelsey. I thought he was better, but he's not. He's wasted. He must've been doing shots or something to get this drunk this quickly.

"Awesome." He barely looks at me. "Thanks, man." He shakes hands with the lead singer.

"Are you okay?"

He stumbles slightly. "Yep, everything's great, Emme. No need to worry about me. Thanks so much for your concern, though."

"What's that supposed to mean?"

He doesn't bother to answer me as he heads to the side of the stage.

"There you are!" Jack screams over the audience. But the second he sees Ethan, he knows we're in trouble. "Dude, are you feeling all right?"

Ethan gives a big smile. "Never felt better!" He runs out to the stage before we're even announced.

"Crap." Jack follows behind him while Ben and I stare at each other.

"Please don't tell me he's been drinking," Ben says.

I shake my head. "Then don't ask a question you don't want to know the answer to."

Ben runs out and I have no choice but to follow him.

Ethan grabs the microphone. "All right, New York City! I'm feelin' good; how are you all doing tonight?" The crowd screams back. Ethan stumbles slightly as he reaches for his guitar. "I'll tell you what. You all look beautiful tonight, you do."

Some girl in the audience shouts, "You're hot!"

Ethan falls to his knees. "Who said that?" There are a bunch of screams. "It's nice to know that somebody appreciates me."

I look back to Jack, who motions for me. I run over.

"Can you do the main riff for 'I Wanna Be Sedated'?" he asks.

"Of course!" I scream over Ethan's incessant banter.

"You might as well do it because I don't think he's going to shut up."

Jack counts off and I start playing.

Ethan starts jumping up and down. This probably isn't the best way to calm him down, but we need to do something to get him focused.

Ethan runs to grab the microphone, but loses balance. Everything plays out in slow motion. He lunges forward, and although he tries to steady himself, he falls down into the small barrier between the crowd and stage.

Ben and I run up to the side of the stage.

When I look down, I see Ethan sprawled out like one of the chalk outlines you see on TV.

I jump down right as I hear voices screaming "Call 9-1-1!" around me.

"Ethan! ETHAN!" I'm afraid to touch him. He isn't responding.

Ethan lies there unconscious with blood dripping from his mouth.

ETHAN

*W*hat the hell is going on?

My head is throbbing and my mouth is dry. No, dry is an understatement — it feels like I drank the Sahara. I try to move my mouth around and feel something sharp.

"Ethan?" I hear a familiar voice in the distance. Emme.

My eyes feel so heavy, but I try to open them. As I move slightly, I feel my right arm encased in something. And a gentle squeeze to my left hand.

"Ethan? It's me, Emme. Please open your eyes."

My eyes flicker open. The effort it takes for such a simple task is exhausting.

I finally open my eyes all the way and it takes a second to soak in my surroundings.

Am I in a hospital? Why is Emme crying? Why is my arm in a cast?

Emme stands up. "Ethan, can you hear me?"

I let out some sort of noise. She lets go of my hand as she runs over to the door. I want to reach out for her. I don't know what's going on, but I want her back.

A nurse comes in, flashes a bright light in my eyes, and checks the machine I'm hooked up to. All I do is stare at Emme, who has tears trickling down her face. I know that I'm responsible for those tears. I wish I knew what I'm supposed to apologize for.

The nurse talks softly to Emme, who nods. Once we're left alone, she picks up a glass of water. "Are you thirsty?"

I nod. Did I lose my voice? Why can't I talk? What is this sharp thing in my mouth? What did I do?

Emme picks up a glass of water and puts the straw to my mouth. The cool liquid feels refreshing, even though I taste something metallic.

"Ethan." Emme grabs my hand and sits down next to me. "I called your parents and they're on the first flight they could get from London. They should be here in a few hours."

I start to cough and she looks panicky. She gets up like she's going to leave, and I grasp her hand so tightly she can't move. She's surprised by my strength.

"Wh . . . What?" I try to get out.

"What happened?"

I nod.

She bites her lip. "Um, to be honest, I don't really know, Ethan. I was sort of hoping you could tell me. Because right before the gig, you disappeared and before we knew it . . ."

The gig. Tyler with Emme.

How do I tell her that I snapped, seeing them together, and tried to find a temporary reprieve to get me through the show? The headlining band had a bottle of vodka and, well . . . I knew it was a big mistake at the time. Clearly, this is one of the few instances when I should've listened to myself.

"During the first song, you were out of control and you fell off the stage and your head hit one of the speakers on the way down. You broke two of your teeth and I guess you reached out to break the fall, but ended up fracturing your arm. It's going to be in a cast for at least six weeks."

Six weeks without being able to play the piano or guitar. I don't even know what this means for school or the band.

"I'm sorry," I finally speak.

Emme's quiet. She looks at the door. "Um, I need to let my mom and the guys know that you're awake now. I don't think the doctors believed for a second that I was your sister, but I wasn't going to let you wake up all alone. But it's six in the morning and . . ."

"Please don't leave me." I feel a tear run down my face.

She hesitates. "Just give me a few minutes."

As soon as she leaves the room, a sense of panic overwhelms me. I've done stupid things. Oh, how I've done stupid things, but I can tell by the way she's looking at me that I've crossed a line I will probably never recover from.

She comes back and sits down. I reach my hand out for her. She takes it. Her eyes are puffy from crying and she looks miserable and exhausted.

"I'm sorry."

She doesn't respond.

"Emme?"

She looks at me.

"I'm sorry."

She nods.

"Please say something to me. Anything."

She closes her eyes and her lips start moving slightly. I'm temporarily relieved that she's doing something that's normal. Any sense of normalcy in this foreign environment is welcome.

She sighs. "Honestly, Ethan, I don't really think I can say what I want to say to you right now. It wouldn't be a good idea."

By the way she won't look at me, I can tell she hates me. But I need to know what she feels. I need to know she can still feel *something* toward me.

"Please, I know you're mad."

"Mad?" She clenches her jaw. "Mad is an understatement, Ethan. I'm furious." Fresh tears start pouring from her eyes. "Do you have any idea what you did? I thought you were dead." Her voice cracks and she buries her face in her hands. "I can't keep watching you do this to yourself. I can't . . . I can't really object to what you do after a show, but before our biggest gig? You had to get wasted? Did you for even one second think about the rest of us before you did such a stupid thing? How much more do you think any of us can take?"

All I could think of was Tyler kissing Emme. An image I wanted to get out of my head as quickly as possible.

"I'm sorry." That's all I can think to say, but I know it isn't enough. Nothing I do will ever be enough. Especially now.

Emme sits there with me for the next few hours as doctors and nurses come in. She has tears in her eyes the entire time. But neither of us says another word.

"Ethan!" My mom breaks the silence when she opens the door and runs to my bedside. "Oh, sweetie, I'm so sorry we're just getting here now. We came as quickly as we could." She looks up and sees Emme. "Thank you so much!" She gives Emme a hug, but Emme doesn't respond. She just heads for the door.

"John!" Mom nudges my dad. "You'd better make sure she gets home okay. It looks like she hasn't slept in days."

I want to run after Emme, call after her, do something. But instead I lie here. In the bed that I made for myself out of self-pity and self-destruction.

One week.

That's how long I'm away from school. Away from the band. Away from Emme.

Everybody comes to visit me — Jack, Chloe, Ben, Mr. North, even Kelsey — but I don't hear from Emme.

I head into class with my arm in a cast and sling.

"Welcome back, Mr. Quinn," Mr. North says to me as I settle into my seat.

"The prodigal jackass returns!" Jack says with a laugh.

Jack and Ben both seemed to have accepted my apologies for my behavior. I know Jack likes to have yet another thing to pick on me for.

"Oh, nice sparkly white teeth, Toothy McGee."

My tongue runs over the caps that were put on the teeth that I broke. If only there were caps to fix everything in life.

Emme walks into class and gives me a halfhearted smile as she sits down.

"Hey," I say to her.

She nods at me.

Mr. North gives us the hour to go over our pieces for next week's concert. The one where I'm supposed to do a killer guitar solo.

Jack gets right to it. "We obviously have a problem with old gimpy here."

Mr. North pulls up a chair beside us. "Listen, guys, we still want you to perform. I discussed with the other department directors, and we are fine if you want to pull a guitar student from the junior class to perform with you."

Jack and Ben start going over different guitarists to fill in for me.

Emme speaks up. "I'm going to do the solo."

"What?" Jack looks surprised.

I smile.

"Find someone to fill in for my rhythm part. I'm going to do the solo."

"Red! That's my girl! Although, I don't mean to doubt you, but it's pretty hard."

Emme glares at Jack. "I can do it."

And the way she says it, there is no question at all that she can.

I'm waiting for Emme at her locker after class.

"I'd say that I don't mean to stalk you, but . . ."

She doesn't look surprised to see me, but she doesn't look pleased, either.

"What's up?" she asks.

I didn't think she was going to acknowledge my existence, so I don't really have a plan.

"We still need to record some more songs for our thesis projects. I wanted to see when, ah, you wanted to come over."

She stares at my sling. "Can you really work the soundboard with your arm?"

"I'm willing to try."

She lets out a small sigh. "I don't know. . . ."

"Please." I feel the desperation seep into my voice and I don't care. I need to fix this. I need Emme. I hate myself so much right now, probably more than she hates me. If that's even possible.

She nods to herself a bit, apparently weighing the pros and cons.

"Hey, guys. Welcome back, Ethan!" Tyler approaches us and I try to look happy to see him. Okay, maybe not happy, but I try to push down the murderous rage I feel inside.

I hold Emme's gaze as Tyler stands between us, looking back and forth, waiting to be acknowledged. Then the corner of Emme's mouth turns up slightly and she tilts her head at me. She looks at Tyler and grabs him by the shirt and kisses him. Hard.

I've never been so jealous of a person (or shirt) in my life.

"Hi," she says as she pushes him away.

His eyes are wide. Clearly not the hello he was expecting.

She can hardly look me in the eye when she finally addresses me. "Yeah, I guess I could come over later. I'll call you."

She and Tyler leave hand in hand.

I feel sick to my stomach.

But I deserve that and so much more.

Emme does come over as promised. But instead of heading to the studio, she sits down on the couch in our living room.

"I'm pretty mad at you, Ethan."

"I know."

She starts playing with the tie that's on her shirt. "But that doesn't excuse me from not returning your phone calls or visiting you while you were out."

I don't even know what to say.

She continues. "I don't know. I felt like I needed to get back at you for what you did. Which is why I made a total fool out of myself today with Tyler in front of you. But I don't really think there is anything that I can do to make you realize what you've done. I want to move on from all of this."

"I'll do anything to make you not hate me."

"I don't hate you."

Part of me doesn't believe her, although I desperately want to.

I sit down next to her and take her hand. "Emme, I will do everything possible to make this up to you, I promise."

She doesn't respond. She slowly pulls her hand away. "There's something I want to show you." She takes out her phone and hands it to me.

I see an e-mail from Juilliard telling her she's been invited to audition in February.

"You did it!"

She gives me a weak smile. This is something she's dreamed about for so long. The old Emme would've been ecstatic, and a feeling creeps up inside me that makes me wonder if I killed that part of her.

"Emme!" I jump up on the couch. "You got invited to audition at Juilliard. JUILLIARD!" I jump right next to her so she starts to shake around.

She stands up. Her eyes get wide. "Flippin' Juilliard!" She jumps up on the couch and lets out the most glorious laugh I've ever heard.

I lose my balance and fall backward onto the couch.

"Ethan!" She lets out a little scream.

"I'm okay!"

She jumps off the couch, slightly out of breath, and sits back down. "I really needed this."

I nod at her. Happy to have Emme back, even if it's temporary.

She turns to me. "I'm sure you'll hear any day."

I pause for a second. "I did hear back."

She swats at my good arm. "You were supposed to tell me!"

"You were the first person I called, but, um, you weren't returning my phone calls."

"Oh." I didn't want to remind her of why she wasn't talking to me. "Well?"

I jump back onto the couch. "Flippin' Juilliard!"

She cheers for me and jumps back on with me to celebrate. We bounce around like idiots for nearly half an hour. I didn't want this moment to end. I'm afraid that the second our feet touch the floor (literally), she'll go back to Upset Emme.

But truthfully, I'll hold on to whatever part of her I can.

Alumni night.

Jack is uncharacteristically pacing around backstage. He finally pulls me aside. "I'm not cool with this. Emme hasn't run through her solo once."

Every time we've practiced, she's stopped playing when the break came for her solo. She's simply said that she's been practicing and knows what she has to do.

I don't doubt for a second that she's ready. Although there's a small part of me that's nervous for her, worried that she might freeze up. I don't know if it's because she got into the Juilliard audition, or she's becoming more comfortable singing her own songs, but Emme's starting to get this quiet confidence about her. I'm more excited for her than anything. I want to see her perform her solo, to finally be the center of attention.

"I don't know, man." Jack folds his arms. "I don't like this. It's like she's suddenly become the unpredictable one. Look at me! I'm a nervous wreck. My hot girlfriend is standing over there in a ridiculously short flapper dress and I can't even enjoy it!" Jack motions toward Chloe, who is getting ready for her twenties dance number.

Jerry Shan, the junior who's playing Emme's part, comes over to me. "Emme looks freakishly calm."

Emme's been standing in a corner, staring at her guitar.

I have no idea why this isn't freaking me out. I, more than anybody, want to see her succeed. Maybe I'm just in denial about how much is at stake once we get on that stage. If it goes poorly, her confidence will be shattered.

Ben joins us. "What's making me nervous is that *you* are calm. *That's* unnerving to me."

"Can everybody relax?" I plead. "Emme is going to rock this out. There's no doubt in my mind."

Okay, maybe there's a tiny fraction of doubt, but I don't think it would help Emme if she saw everybody in the band freaking out.

Jack throws his hands up. "Okay, is this some kind of a joke?

Seriously, *you* are being the voice of reason here? I can't handle this. Please start freaking out."

My laughter just makes Jack more agitated. So I laugh even harder.

Emme walks over. "What's going on?"

"I have no idea. It's like an episode of *The Twilight Zone* over here!" Jack walks away.

"What?" Emme looks confused.

"Nothing." I smile at her. "You're going to be brilliant."

She shrugs. I start to get that familiar nervous feeling I get in the pit of my stomach before we go onstage. But for the first time, it isn't about me. I so desperately want this to go well for Emme.

She gestures at my black long-sleeve shirt. "You can hardly see the sling with that thing on."

I decide to not hold back anymore. I grab her by the waist with my one good arm and kiss her on the forehead.

Before she can respond, we're told to take our places.

Emme is up front with me. Ben is to my right, and Jerry is to Emme's left. Dr. Pafford introduces the eighties by showing famous alumni from that decade. Once the lights come up, I start the opening notes of the song on the keyboard with my one good hand, then Jack comes in with a harder beat than the original.

Emme begins to play the opening riff with such force it feels like the entire audience has been awakened after boring concertos and period dances.

As I start to sing and the crowd begins to move to the beat, I hear cheering from the current students standing in the back. I take the microphone out of the holder. I can't dance and there's no way that I'm going to even attempt it on a song by such an iconic dancer as Michael Jackson, especially with a sling on. I'm doing it because when Emme does her solo, I want her to be alone at the front of the stage.

We come to the break. Jerry plays a few notes as an intro and then it's Emme's turn. I look to her and see her completely calm and composed. And then she starts.

There are no words.

Okay, there are a million.

I see most of the front few rows with their mouths open. Because Emme, the petite redheaded girl of the group, the one who is happy to be background, completely and utterly rips that solo up and throws it on the ground.

I was doing some complicated moves in mine, but she . . .

I'm frozen, transfixed as I watch her fingers move so quickly up the neck of the guitar, hitting notes that I can only imagine in my dreams. I glance back at Jack, whose eyes are practically bulging from his head.

Her guitar screams out for two minutes and it isn't nearly enough. Everybody wants more. I hate it when I come in with the chorus at the end. But nobody can hear me anyway.

Because once Emme hits the final note of her guitar solo, the entire audience erupts in a standing ovation. For prestigious alumni, they sure are one rowdy bunch.

I look over at Emme, who has a small smile as she keeps playing. Her cheeks flush.

I have never been more in awe of her than I am right now.

We finish and I stand near Jack so she gets every ounce of admiration she deserves. She looks back and motions for me to come forward, but I'm not going anywhere.

The lights go down and we all run off the stage. Jack picks Emme up and swings her around.

We hear Dr. Pafford clear his throat. "Well, everybody should be awake now." There is some laughter in the audience. "That was Emme Connelly. Needless to say she is one of our top music students. My sincere apologies to the students who have to follow that."

We all start cheering and celebrating. That is by far the greatest compliment anybody has ever heard from Dr. Pafford.

Emme keeps shaking her head.

"Tell me this, Red." Jack wraps his arms around her. "Why on earth are we letting this one play lead when you can play like that?"

I can't take my eyes off of her. "I totally agree."

Emme stays silent as we're surrounded by dozens of students wanting to congratulate her.

Chloe comes up to me, shock on her face. "Did you have any idea that she could play like that?"

"Yep."

Ben's hands have been over his mouth since we got off the stage. He finally removes them. "Good Lord, Emme. That was seriously hot. I'm sincerely debating changing sides because I want to kiss you on the mouth right now."

Emme laughs. She turns to me. "Ethan, I did it." Her voice is so soft. She almost doesn't believe herself.

In that second, everybody else disappears. I see only her. She is looking at me like she used to when she was happy. Before I screwed everything up.

I know I do stupid things. I do them all the time. I even know when I'm about to do something completely and utterly idiotic. Most of the time I care. But not now. There is only one thing in the world that I care about.

Emme.

I go up to Emme, put my one good hand on her face and kiss her.

On the mouth.

SOPHIE

*J*t's amazing how quickly people forget an inspired performance. I got attention from *A Little Night Music* for less than a week. And now all anybody can talk about is Emme.

She plays the guitar for a song and it's like nothing else happened that night. Of course, I was relegated to the choir for a Motown medley, so I didn't even get the opportunity to do anything.

But not Emme. It's like no girl has ever played the guitar before. And of course Ethan shoving his tongue down her throat afterward, and Tyler running out of the auditorium, gave people even more to talk about.

And do I get any recognition? Of course not.

I just went up to her when we were little and encouraged her to write. And then attend CPA. So why would anybody give me any credit for what's happening to her?

I stare out the window of our practice suite as Emme plays around on the piano. I've been sure to spend more time with her lately. At least maybe she'll remember I exist.

"Hey, Sophie," she says quietly. "Can I talk to you about something?"

"Of course, Emme. Anything!" I run over and sit next to her on the piano bench.

"It's about Ethan. . . . I don't really know what to think about what happened." She looks down and studies her hands.

"I'm sure it was the adrenaline after the performance," I assure her. "I wouldn't make too big a deal about it."

"Really? I guess. Although he's never done anything like that to me before . . . but I don't know. . . ."

"How's it been since after the concert with you two?"

She shrugs her shoulders. "Normal, I guess. I was so shocked about what happened. He quickly apologized and neither one of us has mentioned it since. Jack, of course, gives Ethan grief about it, and then teases me for playing favorites and encourages me to spread the love among the other members."

"And what about Tyler?"

"Oh, well . . . he's pretty mad, but it wasn't like I kissed Ethan. I mean, I don't feel he really has a right to be upset with me."

"Well, you did humiliate him in front of the school."

She looks up at me. "Really? We only went on a few dates, so I didn't think people knew. . . ."

I shake my head. "Emme, people talk. They knew. Poor Tyler. You should really apologize to him. He's a pretty good guy."

Even though he helps Sarah Moffitt. But if Emme is going to be with either Ethan or Tyler, I vote for Tyler. He's truly the lesser of two evils.

"He's really mad. I don't know. . . ."

Gee, Emme is unsure of something? What a shock.

This conversation isn't going anywhere. I pick up the piece of sheet music she's been working on. "What's this?"

"Oh." She takes the paper out of my hand. "Just something new I've been working on."

"For the showcase?"

She bites her lip. "Ah, so nobody knows this . . ."

"You know you can tell me anything, Emme. You're my oldest friend."

She hesitates for a second. "I know. Dr. Pafford called me into his office today."

"What did you do?" This is huge. Dr. Pafford rarely calls students into his office. If he does, it's usually to tell them they didn't pass the audition to attend the next semester.

"He told me that he'd like to see me do a solo audition for the showcase."

"HE WHAT?" I'm so shocked, the words came out too fast. I can tell Emme is taken aback by my reaction. "That's AWESOME, EMME!" I hope I salvage it.

"You think so?" She looks at me hopefully.

They aren't giving out invitations yet and here she's been handed an audition by the principal. And I thought *I* was the one who knew how to play the game.

Well done, Emme, well done.

"I think you'd do a great job. Is that the song you're thinking of doing?"

She looks down at the paper. "I think so. It's still too early to tell."

Maybe Emme isn't as naïve as I thought. Here I thought she was an ally, but now that she's attempting to be a singer, she's becoming part of my competition.

This changes everything.

I exit the studio in a rush, pretending I have somewhere to go, but honestly, I can't think clearly, being in a room with her. As I round the corner toward my locker, I see Ethan struggling with all the stuff he's trying to shove in his backpack with only one functioning arm.

He stops as he sees me, and surprisingly approaches me.

"Have you seen Emme?"

I know I have to do something, anything to put a crack in Emme's perfect world. To put me on top again. I've been fighting tooth and nail to get recognized by Dr. Pafford, but Emme gets everything handed to her. Well, I'm not going down without a fight. There are only so many spots available in the showcase. I can't let her get one that belongs to me.

"Yeah, she's with Tyler. They went that way." I point to the opposite way of the studios.

The mere mention of Tyler's name makes him frown. I can tell that I've hit a nerve.

"They're celebrating. Isn't it great about Emme?"

Ethan says nothing. My day suddenly gets a whole lot better.

"You know, that Pafford invited her to do a solo performance at the showcase. Emme's going solo!" Ethan blinks. "Anyway, I told her I'd join them. Don't they make the cutest couple? I think your little stunt at the concert just made them closer."

I turn on my heel and see Carter standing there with his arms crossed.

"What are you doing?" His face is red.

"Oh, um . . . hey, Carter. I was just leaving!" I grab him by the elbow to walk away, but he pulls my arm off of him.

"Ethan, Emme is not with Tyler. And I don't know why she's talking about Emme going solo."

I cut him off. "You don't know anything. Emme confided in *me*, okay? She's *my* best friend, not yours."

Carter shakes his head. "Yeah, some best friend . . ."

"What's going on, guys?" Emme approaches. She looks between us and I'm frozen. I've got to think fast before everybody turns on me.

"Oh, Emme!" I run up to hug her. "I'm so sorry. It's just that I'm so excited for you, I accidentally let it slip about your solo thing. I'm so proud of you!"

She stands there. "Oh, I . . ." She turns toward Ethan, who looks like he's on the verge of tears. "I was going to tell you. I just don't know if I'm going to do it or not."

Ethan nods. "You should definitely do it. It's what I've been telling you to do all along."

Further proof that Ethan's trying to sabotage me. Why else would he encourage her to go solo?

"Really?" She looks at him with a blinding admiration.

I approach Carter again. "Well, we should really leave the two of them alone."

"That's not all you said."

Why is Carter trying to ruin my standing with Emme?

Emme looks at him. "What?"

Carter stares me down. Emme, clearly confused, looks at Ethan. "What's going on?"

Ethan looks down at the floor. "She said that you're back with Tyler. Is it true?"

"What? I didn't say . . . Sophie?" She looks at me, and I can tell that our friendship is teetering off a steep cliff if I don't fix this.

I can't have Emme hate me. Sure, I want to rattle her before the audition, but I need her song for the showcase.

"Em" — I pull her aside — "I'm so sorry. I was trying to be a good friend. I brought up Tyler to see what Ethan would say. I guess I messed everything up. I'm so sorry. But I think that maybe this gives you an opportunity to talk to Ethan and you guys can clear the air. I'm just trying to help." I give her the best woe-is-me look I can muster.

"That's okay," she says softly.

I give her a big hug, apologize another gazillion times, and tell Carter we should leave them alone.

Shockingly, he agrees to go with me. But he stops as soon as we get outside.

"What was that?" He gestures toward the door.

"Simply a case of too many cooks in the kitchen. There's bound to be some misunderstanding with all those people . . ."

Carter sits down on one of the stone benches that line the front entrance. "You were the only one talking."

"Carter, it's been a long day." I grab his hand. "Let's just —"

He pulls away from me. "I don't know who you are anymore, Sophie. You used to be so kind and considerate, and now you've just gone too far. It was becoming pretty clear to me that you were using me — you aren't the first and you probably won't be the last. But Emme? How can you do that to her? You know she looks up to you and has absolutely no idea how manipulative you are."

I stand up. "Why is it always about her? Huh? Why do you care about Emme? What, do you want to date her now, too? Well, you're going to need to get in line."

"I'm not interested in Emme that way. She's the first person who listened to me and tried to help me, plain old Carter. All you want is your name and photo with Carter Harrison. And I'm not going to play that role any longer. I'm tired by it. I'm tired by your games. I used to think you were special, Sophie, I really did. But now I see the real you and can't believe I put up with it for so long."

I can't believe *he's* breaking up with *me*. That he's doing it now. Before the showcase. Before I'm a star.

"Please, Carter, I'm so sorry. You can't do this to me. . . ."

He gets up. "Good luck with everything, Sophie. I know how much being a star means to you. I just hope you don't ruin too many friendships while you claw your way to the top."

He walks away and I feel deflated.

Why is everything falling apart for me?

How could Carter just break up with me like that?

Like I meant nothing to him. Like I'm nobody.

I'm not just anybody. I *am* special.

I won Brooklyn's Most Talented Kid five years straight.

I've beaten Emme anytime we've had to compete together.

I got a standing ovation during my rendition of "Send in the Clowns."

Okay, so I've made some mistakes. But if there is one thing I know, it's how to get back on top. I can't let everything come crumbling apart because of one little misunderstanding.

Step One: damage control. I pick up my phone and place a call.

"Gossip Guru, this is Stacy."

"Hey, Stacy, it's Sophie Jenkins . . . Carter Harrison's girlfriend."

There's a slight pause. "Oh, hey, Sophie, you guys going out tonight? Would love to get some photographers there."

"No, but I do have a story for you."

I tell Stacy about Carter breaking up with me on the steps of the school (complete with tears) and make sure I give her my name four times.

Step Two: I've got some cupcakes to buy.

Mrs. Connelly is happy to see me as she opens the door to their brownstone. So everything seems normal as I walk into Emme's room. She's lying on her bed, writing out some math problems.

"Emme?" I say softly.

"Oh, hey, Sophie, I wasn't . . ."

I open up a box of cupcakes.

"You didn't need to . . ."

She looks at the cupcakes and I can slowly see the wheels turning in her mind.

"Em, I need to talk to you." I sit on her bed. I let out a sigh. "I don't know what's been going on with me lately. I feel lost. And I haven't wanted to burden you with anything because you've been so busy, but I really need you to know something."

Her eyes are wide as she pats the place next to her for me to sit.

"I don't think I've been a very good friend." She doesn't say anything. "Things haven't been going as I planned at CPA. You know that. I don't know why I've had such a hard time. Sometimes I think it would have been better if I'd stayed in Brooklyn." Tears, *real tears*, sting the corner of my eyes. "But the one thing that I'm glad of, that I'm proud about, is that you went to CPA. It's been amazing to see you grow and shine. I know that I've been so focused on me, and I think you need to know how much your friendship means to me. Not just now, but since we were kids. I remember first seeing you onstage and knowing that I had to meet this insane pianist . . . at eight!

"I know you have a lot going on . . . and I hope that you know you can come to me if you ever need anything. And I don't want us to hang out just when we're rehearsing. You're my friend, my best friend. I miss us just hanging out. And I really feel like you need to know that I'm there for you. No matter what."

"Oh, Sophie." Emme reaches over and gives me a hug.

I finally break down and sob. She holds me and doesn't say anything.

It makes me cry even harder. I can't make myself stop. Because this pain I feel, this hopelessness over my future, is real.

Everything I ever wanted is slipping from my fingertips. My life has started spiraling out of control, and for the first time, I don't know what to do to stop it.

I thought I knew exactly how to become a star. But maybe I don't know anything.

And I hate myself for it.

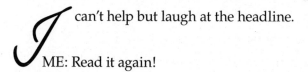

CARTER

I can't help but laugh at the headline.

ME: Read it again!

Mom shakes her head and picks up the paper.

MOM: "Carter Harrison: Heartbreaker."

ME: That's genius. Gossip Guru really is in line for a
Pulitzer this year.

I cross my fingers, and Mom throws the paper down.

I pick it up and start reading about me. It's funny because even
though it's my name and a picture of me from some event a few
months ago, it feels like it's about someone else. My favorite line:

"So be on the lookout, single New York gals. There's another hot bachelor on the loose who has a leading-lady role to fill."

But I have to admit what I love the most is that Sophie is not mentioned by name.

> MOM: I thought once you didn't have a publicist, we didn't have to worry about things like this getting leaked. That Jill would have had a field day with you being single again. Remember her? The one you had before Sheila Marie? The one who leaked your audition to CPA?

I stare at Mom. I thought she leaked . . .

I'm adding this to the list of grave misunderstandings I've had about my mother. I can't believe all these years I've assumed that any press leak was her fault. Or any disagreements she's ever had with producers were because she was a control freak (when actually she was looking out for her child). Or, most importantly, the idea that I'm still an actor is her sole responsibility.

Still, I can't get over how well she's taking the fact that I'm leaving acting. I guess it's not for another three months, but still. *And* she's been really supportive of me looking into art schools.

> ME: Is that why she was fired?

I remember thinking Jill being fired as my publicist had to do with the lack of press coverage my attending CPA was getting.

Anytime there was a mention of it, Mom always commented on it. But I assumed she was unhappy with the placement or something. Not that she was upset that it was mentioned at all.

> MOM: Yes. I made it very clear to her that your education is a private matter. If she wanted to promote the public shows you were in, that was fine, but your classes and personal life were off-limits.

I never even bothered to wonder what my publicist's job was. Mom took care of all that stuff. I did what they told me to do. Something starts to register with her.

> MOM: Who did you think leaked the audition to the press?

I don't say anything.
She picks up the paper and starts to read.

> ME: Mom, when I was little, did I enjoy going on all those auditions?

> MOM: Yes. Every morning, you'd come and sit on my lap and ask me who you were going to be that day. You really seemed to love it. I used to take you to McDonald's after all your auditions because I wanted you to experience something normal — eating greasy

food, playing with the other kids. . . . I didn't really know what else to do. I was a single mother who wasn't planning on having a son with such famous aspirations.

I'm just starting to come to terms with the fact that everything that has happened to me was my responsibility. I'd hate Mom to think that I've painted her as this typical stage mom, because she's anything but.

MOM: Oh, honey, there's a new art exhibit opening at the Guggenheim. Do you want to go next weekend?

Most kids would kill to have such an understanding and supportive parent. I've had one my entire life but have pushed her away. Because it was easier to put the blame on someone else.

But the second I realized that I was the one who was preventing myself from being happy, a whole new world has opened up for me.

I'm happier, more confident, and now, thankfully, single.

And I might be ready to become my truest self.

Since I've, as they say, seen the light, I figure I should pass along the gift of being able to finally see clearly.

Emme studies the menu with such pinpoint focus, you'd think she was memorizing a foreign language.

EMME: Are you sure you're allowed to eat this stuff? I don't see grilled chicken anywhere.

ME: Hey, I do this once a week. I'm letting you into my dirty little sugar underworld. Are you in or not?

EMME: Oh, I'm definitely in. I'm thinking vanilla ice cream —

ME: Boring!

EMME: Let me finish. With peanut butter sauce, hot fudge, caramel, marshmallow topping with whipped cream, almonds, and a cherry, of course.

ME: Of course.

Emme orders a ridiculous sundae from this ice cream shop I discovered a few years ago when I was walking home from the soap's studios in Hell's Kitchen. Now that Chase Proctor has come down with a fever (Spoiler alert! It turns into an incurable disease that leaves me in a coma . . . in case I ever decide to come back), I've been able to keep my shirt on.

We sit down in a corner and she dives in. Lately, she has seemed a little bit more self-assured. I think we all knew that she was special and I'm hoping that maybe she's starting to realize it as well.

ME: So will I still have my arm if I try to get a bite?

Emme has been happily shoving the gooey sundae in her mouth.

EMME: Oops, sorry.

She takes a big spoonful and pushes the rest of the sundae — well, what's left of it — to me. For a little thing, she certainly has a big appetite.

EMME: So, I've been working on my song for the showcase. I think I'm going to audition for it. Do you know what you're going to do?

Senior Showcase audition invitations were issued earlier this week. I wasn't even happy when I got mine.

ME: What do you think the audition board would do if I showed up with one of my paintings?

EMME: That would be wonderful. I really like the one you did of the view of Central Park with the dots.

She starts poking the air with her spoon.

ME: Pointillism.

EMME: Spoken like a true artist.

It's so weird to hear anybody say that about me. An artist.

But this isn't about me. There's something I need to tell Emme.
And I have a feeling — actually, I know for a fact — that this
won't be the first time someone's tried to talk sense into her.

ME: I wanted to talk to you about Sophie.

I can tell by the way that Emme reacts that she's worried that
I'm going to get back together with her. I believe the term *a cold day
in hell* would best describe the possibility of that ever happening.

Better get right to the point.

ME: You know she's using you, right?

Emme drops her spoon and she slouches down in her chair.
Happiness gone, just like that.

> EMME: I know what everybody thinks, okay. I'm not
> that stupid. And don't think that I don't ever get
> upset when she only reappears when she needs
> something, because I do. It really does hurt my
> feelings. But what does everybody expect me to do?
> She is the one who has been singing my songs. I
> never would've had the nerve freshman year to get
> up in front of the school to sing — I don't even know

if I can do it now. So for the past three years, she has given me the confidence to have my songs be heard. I can't just dump her because I'm going to try to sing. I know we aren't the friends we once were, but you have to remember that *I'm* the one who started a band without her. That *I'm* the one who hasn't had a lot of time for her. Not to mention that *I'm* the one that is having ice cream with her ex-boyfriend. So don't put all the blame on Sophie.

She picks up her spoon and scrapes the bottom of the glass.

WAITRESS: Excuse me, Mr. Harrison?

I look to see an older lady with a camera in her hand.

ME: Please, call me Carter.

I flash her the "Carter Harrison" smile. Some roles are hard to forget.

WAITRESS: Would you mind if I took your picture for our wall?

She gestures toward photos of a few local politicians and actors from the studio who grace their walls. I've always noticed it and will admit I often wondered why they never asked before.

But I guess I always came with a baseball hat and hoodie and got my sundae to go. This is the first time I've ever sat down.

ME: Sure.

Emme starts to get up from her seat.

WAITRESS: It's okay. Your little girlfriend can be in the picture.

I smile at Emme, grab her hand before she can protest, and pull her so she's sitting on my lap. We hold up our empty sundae glasses, and the woman gets the photo she needs. She has us both sign the guest book up front and then hands us each a coupon for a free sundae as a thank-you.

EMME: Would it be wrong if I got another one now?

I pull her outside and we start walking back toward school. I figure now is as good a time as any.

ME: So there's something else I want to talk to you about.

EMME: I really don't want to talk about Sophie anymore. Or Ethan, for that matter. All everybody wants to do is to talk about that stupid kiss. It was just the high from performing. Believe me when I say that I've seen him kiss a lot of girls after a show. *A lot.* It isn't the big deal that everybody is making it out to be. I just happened to be the closest person next to him.

And here I thought *I* was the one playing pretend.

ME: No, it's not that. It's about school.

EMME: Oh, um, sorry.

ME: That's okay. It's just, I think . . . I think if I can't transfer to the art program, I'm going to drop out of CPA.

The words just hang out there. I turn to study Emme as she walks. She starts nodding slowly and I can tell she's planning her next words carefully.

EMME: Dropping out of high school really isn't the best idea, Carter.

ME: I know. It isn't high school; it's CPA. I'm tired of having all these acting roles forced on me. If I can't do art, there's no reason to be there. I can take the GED — that's what I was going to do when I was being taught on the set. So I don't really need to have my diploma from CPA, especially since it would mean keeping up the Carter Harrison Acting Charade. I've been acting for as long as I can remember. It's not something I want to do anymore. I'm really sick of living a lie, doing things that don't make me happy.

Emme and I walk to the park and I talk. Not lines that have been written for me, but what I've wanted to say for years.

So for the first time since I can remember, I let it all out. My frustrations with school, the teachers, the principals, how CPA really hasn't been what I thought it would be. That I need so much more. That I deserve so much more. I want to be happy. I want to create art, real art, not recite cheesy lines.

I decide to not hide behind a role or pretend to be someone that I'm not. Instead, I do the one thing that terrifies me more than anything. I drop the act. I just be.

I believe the saying is "The truth shall set you free." But what they don't say is that once you unleash one shackle that's been holding you down, you want them all freed.

I wait outside Dr. Pafford's office. And I'm not even nervous. I know what I'm about to do might be considered crazy to some, maybe even a little self-destructive, but I figure it's worth a shot.

Dr. Pafford's secretary lets me know he's ready to see me.

DR. PAFFORD: Carter, so great to see you. We're all looking forward to your audition for the showcase!

He shakes my hand. I sit down in the chair opposite his desk.

ME: That's what I'm here to talk to you about.

DR. PAFFORD: Would you like my thoughts on your audition piece? I think you do such a great job with Arthur Miller's work.

Here goes nothing. I take out my portfolio and unzip it and place several of my art pieces on his desk.

ME: I was hoping that I could be considered for some of my art pieces instead of acting.

His eyes politely roll over my work and he leans back in his chair.

DR. PAFFORD: You are part of the drama department, Mr. Harrison. The showcase is to highlight the work of the different departments in the school, not a student's outside hobby.

To be honest, I saw that coming. But that's not the real reason why I'm here, so I decide to stop stalling.

ME: I understand. I was wondering if I could audition to be part of the art department next semester. I know I would only be eligible for the beginners' classes.

DR. PAFFORD: There's no transferring of programs this late in the process. You are graduating after next semester . . . in drama.

ME: Well, I have enough credits that I was wondering if —

DR. PAFFORD: Mr. Harrison, you are here to act. That is the program you enrolled in. You cannot shift to a new program after three and a half years.

ME: I see. Well, thank you for your time.

I get up to leave.

DR. PAFFORD: Now about that audition piece — what are you going to perform?

I turn toward him.

ME: I'm not auditioning. It's been an incredible experience here, Dr. Pafford. But I have no desire

to continue to be part of something I don't
believe in.

I can tell that he doesn't know how to respond.
He clears his throat and finally speaks.

DR. PAFFORD: I'm sorry to hear that.

I look closely at him.

ME: I'm not.

I head to my locker and grab all my personal belongings. I
don't even hesitate for a second as I walk out of the school and
don't look back.

Yes, the truth shall set you free.

EMME

*E*verything seems to be happening all at once.

I knew that senior year would be overwhelming, but the next two weeks are like a perfect storm: Senior Showcase auditions, finals, and auditions for second semester. I'm thankful Ethan's cast finally came off a few days ago so the band is back to full strength. I even had a chance to talk to Tyler; he was nice enough to listen to everything I had to say, but I don't think he wants anything to do with me after that "humiliation." I guess I don't blame him.

But of course with everything coming up, all anybody really wants to talk about is Carter.

I couldn't believe Carter actually dropped out of CPA. But he looked so happy when he told me about it. He was done with pretending and he was going to take some time off to focus on what he wants.

I guess I've been really lucky to always know what I want to do: music. I'll admit the uncertainty of where I'll be next year is stressful, but as I walk into the rehearsal room and see Jack, Ben, and Ethan, I know I'm not alone in this.

Jack gives me a smirk and cocks one eyebrow. "Well, hello, *Emma*."

"Hi." I continue to tune my guitar, not sure what Jack is trying to get at.

"So, *Emma*, anything you'd like to share with the band?"

Ben takes the bait. "What are you blabbering about, Jack? And why are you calling her Emma?"

Jack laughs. "I guess you haven't read all about it, huh?" Jack pulls up something on his phone, and Ben gasps.

"What?" I go up and pull Jack's phone from his hand. On the screen is the photo taken at the ice cream parlor of me on Carter's lap. The caption reads: *Harrison with girlfriend Emma days before he left the prestigious CPA.*

I scroll up and start reading the gossip site's article about Carter's departure from CPA. The article paints Carter as some diva who was causing problems at school and decided to drop out. The only thing they have right is that he's taking a vacation. He and his mom left for Italy yesterday for a few weeks. Then when he gets back he's going to take the GED and enroll in art classes. But leave it to the Gossip Guru to "report" only on hearsay from students at CPA who didn't like Carter, let alone know him.

"Well?" Jack's been studying me.

"Well what?" I reply. What happened with Carter isn't anybody's business.

"You're now dating Carter Harrison?" Jack folds his arms. "Because really, Red — oh, I'm sorry, *Emma* — you certainly seem to be getting around these days. You're going to have to have a separate binder just to keep track of your social life."

"No, we were having ice cream and the place wanted a picture. . . . I don't know why they have my name as Emma. Or why —"

My stomach drops. Tyler is going to hear about this and any ounce of hope I had that he'd forgive me someday has disappeared. But even worse, there's no way Sophie isn't going to see this and think that I'm with Carter now.

"I've got to make a phone call." I run out of the room and call Sophie. She doesn't answer, so I leave a babbling message explaining everything. She hasn't really talked about Carter since their breakup, but I have a feeling she'd be more upset with the fact that I'm in a picture, and identified, even incorrectly, on her favorite gossip site.

They're waiting for me when I return.

Jack laughs. "You know, Red, I never figured you to be the biggest player in the group. First Tyler, then Ethan, now Carter. Pretty impressive."

Ethan glares at Jack. Leave it to Jack to once again blow Ethan's kiss after our performance completely out of proportion.

Jack is blissfully unaware of the daggers Ethan is shooting him so he continues. "I guess it is a good thing that I'm taken; I don't think my heart could take your games."

Ethan taps the microphone. "Are we ready?"

We all pick up our instruments and run through a few chords, but before we start, Ethan interrupts us.

"I've been thinking that maybe we should redo this song as a duet."

He looks at me.

I shake my head. "No, I think it's way better if you sing it alone."

"You know everybody is going to hear you sing at the show-case anyway?"

"Yeah, that's not guaranteed. I was asked to do a solo based on my guitar playing, not my singing."

Ethan gives me a knowing smile. "You do realize that Dr. Pafford and the entire audition panel have heard you sing when you audition each semester. It's not like they've never asked someone to audition before, Emme. They know exactly what they are doing."

The thought of performing at the showcase by myself has left me a nervous wreck. I don't like thinking about it. To be honest, I was thankful to Carter for opening up to me. And to Sophie for practicing her song. And of course, the guys. I have every confidence that I'll be on that stage that evening with the guys and with Sophie. But being there by myself, I don't think I can do it.

"I think we should leave the song as it is," I state, and start strumming my part. Jack takes the hint and starts playing along with me, and then we are a band. One unit, playing while Ethan sings by himself.

That's the way it should be.

It's gotten even worse.

My hands are shaking. If I can't perform in front of Ethan, then there's no way that I'm going to be able to do this on Friday.

I'm sitting at the piano in Ethan's house, putting the final touches on my new song for the showcase. Ethan's heard me sing a lot lately since we've been recording our albums for our senior thesis.

But there's something about this new song that makes me uneasy. Probably because the entire time I wrote it, I didn't have the comfort of knowing that Sophie would be singing it. It would be me up there. And of course it ends up being the most personal thing I've ever written.

Ethan can tell I'm stalling. "All right, let's go for a walk."

We leave his apartment building and head west. The air has gotten colder and Christmas lights are decorating the streetlights and shops. Ethan doesn't say much, but as soon as we hit Columbus Circle, I know where he's taking me.

We walk up Broadway, past the turn we'd take to go to school, and a few more blocks north. We get to Sixty-fifth Street and walk past the main Juilliard building, pause in front of Alice

Tully Hall, the main performance venue for the school. We walk up some stairs to Lincoln Center Plaza and sit on the edge of the fountain.

Ethan finally breaks his silence. "Have you thought at all about what happens if we both get in?"

I shrug. I honestly can't wrap my head around what will happen if I get in.

"You know, you sell yourself short. A lot. And it is beyond devastating." I look up and see him studying me. He wraps his arms around himself. "You're the most selfless person I've ever known. You drop everything to help Sophie, you don't even hesitate to encourage Carter to go after his dreams, you've been nothing but supportive of Jack, Ben, and me. But you can't ever do it for yourself."

I'm silent. I don't know what to say.

"I just wish, for even a second, that you could see yourself through my eyes. Or through anybody else's for that matter. And you know how after the whole 'Beat It' thing, everybody was so surprised? Well, I wasn't. I knew all along that you were going to do it. Granted, I don't think my mind was capable of imagining what you did do, but it was astonishing. *You're* astonishing, Emme."

I feel my cheeks burn. Ethan keeps looking at me and I can't meet his eyes. I can't. I look down and study my shoes. I know I have to say something.

"Thanks. Really, thanks, Ethan." I continue to stare out at the pedestrians crossing the plaza, anything but look at Ethan. "I just . . . you have to understand that my entire life, I've been the person behind the person, you know? I've never had the desire to be in the spotlight, to have the attention on me. I've wanted to make music, that's it."

Ethan places his hand on top of mine. "Is it that you never had the desire, or were you told to stand back?"

I pull my hand away. "I should've known that it was going to end up coming back to Sophie."

He sighs. "It always does, doesn't it? It's always about her."

My patience has worn thin about everybody questioning Sophie. She's singing one of my songs for the showcase audition. I'm not giving her a kidney.

He gets up and stands right in front of me, so I have no choice but to look at him.

"It kills me that you always put yourself second to her. She's not worth it, and I wish that you would see how special *you* are. What terrifies me is that you're going to throw it all away for someone who isn't worth you. There are few people who are — believe me, I know I'm not. Just please, Emme, for yourself, stop drinking the Kool-Aid."

I don't say anything. I'm so tired of having to defend Sophie to everybody else in my life. Or maybe it's because I know he has a point. Although after everything Ethan has pulled, he really doesn't have the right to be judging anybody.

"It's getting late. . . ." I get up and start to walk to the subway. Ethan follows me, but we don't say another word to each other the entire time.

★ ★ ★ ★ ★ ★ ★ ★ ★ ★ ★ ★ ★ ★

Two days away from the showcase auditions. All of our studio classes have been turned into practice sessions.

Sophie and I are in one of the piano suites, going over her song.

"It's sounding so great, Em." Sophie gives me a little squeeze.

One thing I wish Ethan, Carter, pretty much anybody would understand is that Sophie has been so nice about the mix-up of me being photographed and identified as Carter's girlfriend. Once I told her my side of the story, everything was fine. I was really expecting a ton of drama, but she believed me and hasn't brought it up since.

Now we're focused on doing the best audition we can. We go through the song a couple more times. Sophie looks satisfied after making some notes on her lyric sheet.

"I'm going to run to the bathroom and maybe get some tea." She pats her throat. "Want anything?"

I tell her I'm good, and before the door even closes, her phone, which she left on top of the piano, buzzes, and her screen comes alive with a text.

"Oh, Sophie!" I grab her phone and call after her, but she's already down the hall.

I quickly glance at the phone and freeze as I see my name is mentioned in a text from Amanda. I set the phone down. I shouldn't look.

But I can't help it.

I pick up the phone and see Amanda's text.

Tell Emme the Needy I say HI. Hang in there!

Emme the Needy?

Amanda calls me that? I can't believe that Sophie would let her. . . .

I know I shouldn't do it. That I'm a horrible person for doing so, but I touch the screen and the entire back-and-forth from Sophie and Emme scrolls out in front of me.

Sophie: Off to see E. Ugh.

Amanda: Just a few more months and then U don't have to deal w/ her.

Sophie: June can't come soon enough. Can't believe I have to spend an hour kissing up 2 her.

Amanda: NP for an awesome actress like U. ☺

Sophie: She really thinks she can get a spot at the SS. Delusional much? Gah, she's here. Barf.

Then there's Amanda's last text. I think I'm going to be sick.

I run out of the suite and head in the direction opposite to the bathroom. I need privacy. I run past a row of the practice suites, fighting back tears.

"Hey," Tyler says to me as I rush past. I can barely even nod at him. He deserves more than that from me, but at this moment, I can hardly breathe. I turn the corner and search for an empty practice suite.

"Emme?" I hear Ethan call out my name. I turn around to see his head poking out of one of the rooms.

I burst into tears. He runs over and grabs me by the hand and leads me into the tiny solo room where he was practicing. He leans me against the closed door so nobody can see me.

"Is everything okay? Are you all right?" His eyes are filled with panic.

I'm sobbing so hard I can't speak. I shake my head.

"What can I do? What do you need?" He looks around the room like there is something that can help me.

But there's nothing. The realization of what everybody has been saying hits me.

I'm a fool.

I stop crying and just stare at the wall. How can Sophie say those kinds of things behind my back? Such hurtful things. Even though our relationship has changed, I thought we were still at least friends. Maybe not best friends, but with all the history we share, how can she look herself in the mirror after treating someone like this?

"Emme?" My silence freaks out Ethan even more.

He's wiping my tears away and then starts rubbing my shoulders. This isn't the first time he's had to comfort me while I sob uncontrollably.

Sophomore year: Sophie invited me to go to a Broadway show, then two days beforehand canceled on me, saying she couldn't make it. Although Gossip Guru ran an article about

Carter Harrison going to that play, and even though his date's arm was cut off in the picture, I recognized Emme's music charm bracelet. That's how I found out they were dating.

Junior year: I spent three weeks helping Sophie get ready for her audition for *Grease*. I fell behind in a few classes since Sophie wanted to practice her routine two hours a night. I was with the guys when we ran into Sophie and Amanda celebrating Sophie's role as Frenchy. She didn't call me or text me or even tell me she got the part. Instead she went out with Amanda.

"Emme, please say something; you're scaring me," Ethan pleads.

I look at him and see how much he cares about me. Out of the thousands of students in this entire school, I'm so glad he found me.

Then it hits me.

"Ethan?"

"Yes." I don't think he's breathing.

"You're my best friend."

He lets out a little laugh. "*That's* why you're so upset? The realization that *I'm* your best friend?"

I shake my head. Then I tell him about what happened. He tries to pace back and forth, but the room's too small. So he just shakes his knee while I repeat the texts. (I don't think those words will ever be erased from my memory.)

After it comes out, I sit down in his chair. Exhausted.

He kneels down beside me. "I don't have to tell you about my feelings for Sophie, but Emme, I'm truly sorry. Especially that this was the way you had to find out. You didn't deserve this. You know that, right?"

I think back on everything I've done for Sophie. I have no doubt that we were truly close friends once. That the friendship we had as kids was real. But then we came to CPA and things changed. I didn't want to believe it, and I held on to something that wasn't there for so long. I wanted to believe that things were still the same, but they weren't.

I kept making excuses for Sophie even though I knew she was using me. I let her do it because I was too scared. I needed to hide behind her.

But maybe this is the push I need to finally stand center stage.

"Yeah, I know."

Ethan gets back up. "Stay here. I need to go do something."

Whoever said that people don't change was full of it.

That or they never had a friend who wanted to be famous.

SOPHIE

Where the hell is Emme? I go to use the restroom and she disappears?

I'm waiting around for five more minutes and then I'm going to leave. I know that I'm going to nail that audition on Friday anyway.

I hear the door open. About time.

I turn around and see Ethan.

Great.

"Hey, Ethan, have you seen Emme?" I say sweetly to him. It kills me since I know he doesn't like me, but I'd die to sing one of his songs. Okay, not die, but be nice to him and that's bad enough.

He grabs my phone out of my hand.

"Excuse me?"

He smiles at me. "I'm answering your question. You want to know where Emme is, here's your answer."

He hands me back my phone and it's showing Amanda's texts.

"This is my personal property. How dare you —"

"Emme knows."

"What? You violate my privacy and have the gall to come in here and say things like *Emme knows*. What, has she figured out that you have some sick obsession with her?"

"She saw the texts. She knows that you are not the friend you've been pretending to be this entire time. She finally sees who you really are."

I can't believe that Ethan and Emme think they have the right to go through my stuff and then get mad at *me*. Are they even serious?

"How did she see the texts? You know what, it doesn't even matter. I can explain."

Ethan laughs. "This I'd love to hear." I want to punch that smug look on his face.

I try to think. This can't be happening two days before the audition. I knew that Ethan would try to find a way to sabotage my spot in the showcase.

"Amanda is very sensitive about all the time I spend with Emme. . . ."

"Right, Amanda, who you've known for two years, thinks she should get priority over Emme, who you've known since you were eight and is the only reason why anybody wants to hear you perform. It's for her songs, but, please, do go on. . . ."

Ethan's such a pompous jerk. He and Emme deserve each other.

"You know what? I don't owe you anything. Where's Emme?"

"She's gone."

Whatever. All I need to do is apologize to Emme and all will be forgiven.

And I need to put a password on my phone.

I go to leave, but Ethan blocks the door.

"Do you have any idea how much you've hurt her? And not just today, but how many times I've had to literally wipe the tears away from her eyes because of something you've done? Since the day I met her, Emme has done nothing but praise you and run herself ragged to help you out. What have you ever done for her? Nothing. I almost hoped that I was wrong about you, for Emme's sake."

"Oh, please, it's like Emme is the poor little lost soul who does no wrong."

"No. Emme is an extraordinarily talented person with the biggest heart. She's just been beaten down enough to think that she doesn't belong in the spotlight. Because her supposed best friend pushed her back while taking something that doesn't belong to her. Well, your time's up. Stay away from Emme. You've done enough damage."

He walks out of the room.

Ethan thinks he knows everything, but I know Emme. Everything is going to be fine.

She'd never let me down.

★ ★ ★ ★ ★ ★ ★ ★ ★ ★ ★ ★ ★ ★

I'm trying not to panic, but Emme is giving me the silent treatment. I've called and texted, but she isn't getting back to me. I can understand why she'd be mad about what happened today, but if she wants to make it in showbiz, she needs to toughen up. People in the business are going to say way worse things about you during auditions.

Really, when you think about it, I'm doing her a favor.

I head up the steps of her family's brownstone. It seems that I have to do my groveling in person. I knock on the door, but from the look I get from Mrs. Connelly, I can tell that the cupcakes I have aren't going to be enough.

"Hi, Sophie," she says coolly.

"Hi, Mrs. Connelly. Can I speak with Emme?"

She shakes her head. "She's not here. She's spending the rest of the week in the city at a friend's."

I can't believe that her mom would let her stay at Ethan's. That's where she has to be. Ethan is keeping guard over her.

"Oh. Well, I guess I'll see her at school tomorrow. Thanks!"

I turn around and head the few blocks to my house. I want to think that this will blow over, but if Ethan has his fortress around Emme, there's no way he's going to let me get in.

Desperation starts to sink into every pore of my body. I have to think of something to do. And fast.

I'm waiting by her locker in the morning. She sees me and gives me a weak smile. But still, a smile.

Good old reliable Emme. I know I've been going a little crazy lately. My mind is continually racing with different scenarios, but maybe I'm just overreacting. I can fix this. I've always been able to make things fine between the two of us. Okay, so maybe I haven't been the greatest friend to her lately, but she knows how much I need this. It's not only my last shot, but the most important one.

"Hey, Em, listen, I'm a jerk, and I need to tell you about what happened."

She nods. "It's okay. You don't need to explain."

Oh, wow. I didn't . . .

I give her a huge hug. "Oh, man, if I haven't told you lately how awesome you are, you are awesome! Our audition time tomorrow is one fifteen."

"Sophie . . ." She looks at me with confidence, no biting of the lip, nothing. This can't be good. "You've been one of my closest friends since I was eight. And I've learned a lot about friendship lately and I know that friends should always be there for each other. Friends also love one another unconditionally . . ."

I feel such relief. I haven't lost her, after all.

". . . and understand when a friend has to make a difficult decision. I've never had to test a friendship, never had a reason to question one before . . ."

Uh-oh.

". . . but I'm not going to be accompanying you tomorrow. I can't stop you from using my song, but I won't be providing you with the accompanying music. If you are truly my friend, you'll sing another song . . . and still want to talk to me."

This is a test. I know she's testing me.

"Of course, Emme. I understand. I really wish you'd let me tell you my side of the story, but you're right. True friends are unconditional and I love you regardless of whether you're by my side tomorrow."

I give her a hug. She just stands there as I wrap my arms around her.

"Um, okay," I say. "Well, I guess I'll see you later. Bye!"

I walk away from her and my legs start shaking. What am I going to do tomorrow if she doesn't come through for me? I guess I could have Amanda play . . . the song we did at the beginning of the year. But the new one is so much better.

This is a disaster.

No, I know this is a game she's playing with me.

Fine, I'll play her game.

All day. All freakin' day I'm waiting to hear from Emme. For her to tell me that I've passed her stupid test. Every time I see her in between classes, I wave at her and smile. I decide to hunt her down after school.

"Oh, hey, guys!" I try to pretend that I hadn't been walking in circles for twenty minutes as I wait for Emme to appear at her locker. Of course her guard dog is right next to her.

"Hi, Sophie." While she greets me, it doesn't have the same

kindness as it usually does. She pulls out her books and studies them. Ethan leans against the locker and smiles at me.

"Um, I saw your mom yesterday and she mentioned that you're staying in the city for the week?"

She nods. "Yep, have lots to do."

"Oh, okay. Um . . ."

I can't take this anymore. If she doesn't accompany me tomorrow, I won't get in the showcase. If I don't get in the showcase, talent scouts won't discover me. If the talent scouts don't discover me, I won't get a record contract. No record, no Grammy. This is it. Doesn't she see she is ruining my last chance? Without this I have nothing. *I'm* nothing.

Emme was the only part of my Plan that was working. I can't have this fall apart, too.

"Emme, please, please . . ." The tears spilling out are real. I need this. It kills me that I need her to do it, but I do. "You know I can't do this without you. You know it, why won't you help me? Why would you abandon me when I need you the most?"

Emme shuts her locker. "Ethan, can you give us a few minutes?"

Ethan opens his mouth, but thinks better of it and closes it. Thank God.

When it's just the two of us, Emme launches in. "I've been wondering something, Sophie. Why do you hate me?"

"I don't — how could you . . ."

"No, I've been thinking about it. What you said to Amanda, how you've acted toward me for the last couple of years. You ignored me the entire summer, but once a mention of an audition comes up, we're suddenly best friends again. You've never once come to any of the band's gigs, yet I go to every performance of yours, even when you're in the chorus. You know what I think? You don't like me getting attention. I even think about when we were twelve and you convinced me to dye my hair brown. It hit me last night. You don't like that I have hair that makes people look at me and not you."

She ruffles her bright red hair. I hate that hair.

"Not one time have you ever encouraged me to do something that doesn't somehow affect you. What kind of friend is that?"

I've had enough. I get in her face. "What kind of friend abandons someone at the most important time of their life? What kind of person does that make you?"

She backs away from me. "I'm putting myself first. I guess that makes me just like you."

She walks away and leaves me in the hallway. Alone. I'm all alone.

I want to scream. But I can't. I need my voice for tomorrow. I want to scream at Emme, at the world, but mostly, right now I want to yell at Amanda.

She fumbles over a few chords.

I try to keep my voice even. "That's not how it goes." I sing a few more lines for her and she shakes her head.

"I can't figure out an accompany part just from your vocals."

"Emme could."

Amanda stands up at the mention of her name. "Yeah, well, then get her to do it. It's almost midnight, and we need to go back to the song from the first day of school. She wrote out that part. Or we can do something else — Sarah Moffitt isn't doing an original song. She'll do some Broadway number. *Or* we can do one of my songs."

Ugh. Amanda's songs are terrible. All she does is rhyme *girl* with *world* and thinks that constitutes lyrics.

"Fine. We'll do the old Emme one." I grab the song she wrote for the freshman welcome performance.

An old song is better than no song.

I get to the hallway where everybody is lined up for the auditions. The dance, art, and drama department members went this morning. This afternoon is vocal and instrumental music. I take a few deep breaths and see Emme sitting by herself, her hands in her lap.

My heart practically jumps out of my chest when I see her.

"Emme!" I pretty much squeal at the sight of her. She gives me a smile.

I knew it. She'd never let me down.

I know I say this a lot, but this time I mean it. She's a good friend. And I'm an awful friend. But I'll find a way to thank her. I'll make it up to her somehow.

"I knew you'd be here, I knew it."

"Sophie!" I hear Amanda call out.

I ignore her.

"I just need you to know that —"

Mr. North pokes his head into the hallway. "Okay, we are running a few minutes behind. Sarah Moffitt, you're up, then Emme Connelly. Let's go!"

She's here for herself.

I'm so mad at Emme, I want to rip her hair out of her head. But then I remember, she's not as tough as me. If she's going to ruin my chances of getting into the showcase, I'm going to return the favor.

"Oh, I forgot about your little attempt to steal the spotlight. Yeah, good luck."

She turns and smiles at me. "Thanks!"

I get in her face. "God, I was being sarcastic. It's laughable that you think you can waltz in and become a singer. Sure, you're an incredible, amazing songwriter. But I've heard you sing, and your voice is nothing special. Never has been, never will be. Here's the thing you need to realize: A bad singer can ruin a good song, but a good singer can make any song better. So let's be clear on who's been doing who a favor all these years — it's me, the voice. But I guess we're both about ready to get that proof when you fall flat on your face in there. So really, good luck."

The color starts to drain from her face.

Her name is called out.

She hesitates, but then leans in. "You know, Sophie, I came here today with every intention of accompanying you. I didn't want to have that on my conscience. But thank you, really, thank you for being honest with me for once."

She walks into the audition room.

My mind races to try to see what I can do. But it's useless. When she comes out of the room, she has a huge smile on her face and she races past me. I see her getting picked up by Ethan, with Ben and Jack there to congratulate her.

Everything swirls around me. I think I'm going to be sick. It's the biggest moment of my life and she ditches me. And people think that *I'm* the bad friend?

Amanda puts her arm around me. "You don't need her."

I take a deep breath. I know I can do this. No, I don't need Emme.

My name is called out and I walk into the room. I wish we could go with a different song. I don't want to owe Emme anything. Because she is nothing to me. She has gotten me as far as I needed her to.

The rest is up to me.

ETHAN

*E*xams are over, second semester auditions finished.

    There's only one thing left before we're freed for winter break.

The entire senior class is in the auditorium awaiting our fates.

I wish we could just look at a list, but leave it to Dr. Pafford to want to create even more drama.

He steps to the podium and starts going over the lineup for the Senior Showcase. All of the usual suspects are named — Trevor Parsons, Zachary David, Sarah Moffitt — and I hold my breath. I'm not worried about the band making it, but I want Emme to get in so bad. Her song is better than anything I've ever written.

I'd hate to think what not getting in would do for her confidence, especially before her audition for Juilliard.

I'm staring down Dr. Pafford, trying to will him to say Emme's name.

My hands are balled up in fists. I'm so tense, I nearly jump when Emme touches my hand.

She whispers in my ear. "It's going to be fine, Ethan. Really, I'm going to be okay no matter what." I get goose bumps from her breath on my neck.

Dr. Pafford clears his throat. "This leaves us with one spot left."

Only one spot? He hasn't mentioned either the band, or Emme, or Sophie.

I will lose all faith in humanity if Sophie is chosen over Emme.

The entire room is silent. Anytime we've had a featured performance, it has always gone to Carter — no questions asked. And now with him out of the running, that spot is up for anybody. Truthfully, I sort of assumed the band would get it. I think everybody does.

I grab Emme's hand. I know how much being in the showcase would mean to Jack and Ben, but I want her in it. It needs to be Emme.

Dr. Pafford finally continues. "We are going to do something different this year. Our final, featured spot will showcase two songs. First, Emme Connelly, Jack Coombs, Benjamin McWilliams, and Ethan Quinn performing an original song by Mr. Quinn, and then Miss Connelly will end with her song."

There is some applause, mostly from the other students who made the showcase. Jack and Ben get up and start celebrating, but Emme just sits in her seat.

"Red! Come here!" Jack has to pick Emme up off her seat to give her a hug.

She smiles at him, but it seems forced.

I take Emme by the hand and lead her out of the auditorium.

Jack is more than happy to be the representative of the band to receive the congratulations for our spot.

"Emme? You know it freaks me out when you go all comatose on me."

She blinks quickly like she's trying to wake up.

"It's my fault Sophie didn't get in."

It kills me that in one of her most triumphant moments, one that every other senior is envious of, she's thinking about Sophie.

She takes a deep breath. "Sorry, you know that my Kool-Aid detox is going to take a while. She made it very clear what she thinks of me. It's for the —"

Emme looks like she's seen a ghost. I turn around and see Sophie, a very angry and tear-soaked Sophie approaching. I stand in front of Emme trying to block her, protect her.

Sophie practically runs up to us and pushes me out of the way.

"You!" She gets in Emme's face. "You've ruined my life! Are you happy now?"

The other students exiting the auditorium start gathering around. I want them to all go away — Emme doesn't need this. She doesn't deserve this.

I gently move Emme back so I get in between them.

"It's not Emme's fault, Sophie. Quit blaming your failures on her."

"Shut it, Ethan! God, you're so desperate and pathetic. She only sees you as a friend. The only person she's interested in screwing around here is me!"

Her words sting. I try to block them out of my mind, but up until a week ago, Emme did think that Sophie was her best friend. She would've told her what she thinks of me. Not that I ever truly thought that Emme would ever see past my mistakes and want to be with me.

The tension in the air is so thick. My mind races to find what to say.

I feel Emme's hand on the small of my back and she moves me aside.

"Sophie," she says in a calm, controlled voice, "don't you dare talk to Ethan like that. He's been a true friend to me, unlike you."

"Yeah, a true friend who wants to get in your pants."

There's some laughter. I can't believe she said that in front of practically the entire senior class.

Plus, that's not true. I want more than that from Emme.

Not that I haven't thought about what it would be like . . . every moment of every waking (and dreaming) hour.

Emme stands up tall, but I see her body is twitching. She takes a deep breath. I've only seen her like this one other time, and it was when she gave me a tongue-lashing that still stings to this day. I thought I never wanted to see that side of her again.

But with Sophie being on the receiving end, it couldn't happen soon enough.

"I can't believe it has taken me this long to see what you're really like. Since you feel the need to air dirty laundry in front of everybody . . ." She motions to the nearly one hundred people standing around. "Guess what. When I write songs for you, I have to limit the melody to ten notes because those are the only notes you can hit well. You don't have good range, which is what your problem is. I've known that for years, but I've hidden it. That's why you only shine when you sing *my* songs, because I've been trying to help you . . . by disguising your biggest flaw. Well, one of your flaws. You can't blame me for your lack of range. You can't blame me for you not getting into the showcase. You always want things to be all about you. Anytime I come to you with a problem, you don't want to hear it, unless it has to do with you."

Emme's face is bright crimson. I can see tears starting to well up in her eyes.

"Well, congratulations, Sophie — you finally got what you wanted. Because this, not getting into the showcase, is all about you. You struggling in class, it's all about you. The wake of relationships you've destroyed to get to this moment, it's all on you.

Enjoy your moment. You've earned everything that's coming to you. Truly."

Emme grabs my arm and starts to walk away. There's some muttering and applause as she leaves.

I try to think of what to say to her, but I can't. Yet again, I'm completely at a loss for words. And always at the worst times.

"Please don't say anything — just keep walking." Her voice is quivering and she's sniffling.

It seems that this is one of the few moments in my life where being an idiotic mute is working in my favor.

She leads me up to the practice suites and enters one of the small rooms and closes the door behind us.

She doesn't say anything. She just looks at me. We both sit there in silence and stare at each other. I'm resisting every urge in my body to grab her, hold her, kiss her.

Emme opens her mouth and lets out an agonizing sob. She collapses on the floor.

I rush to her side and hold her, willing myself to say something, anything to comfort her. All I can do is cradle her in my arms and run my fingers through her hair. Everything I want is right here, so close to me, but I can't seem to find my voice.

Emme pulls me away and starts to wipe away her tears. "I'm sorry, Ethan." She has trouble catching her breath. "I'm so sick of crying. It's just, I can't believe how much I've been used, been betrayed by someone I thought was my friend."

She wraps her arms around her legs and starts rocking back and forth. "I feel so alone."

Those words feel like daggers. How can she feel alone when I'm right here? I'm always here for her. I always have been.

A loud voice starts screaming in my head, *Then tell her that! Tell her how you feel! Tell her now, you imbecile!*

"It's like every person I decide to trust lets me down."

You would never hurt her! Open up your mouth and tell her that!

She looks up at me as if she realizes what she just said. "I'm sorry, I'm so sorry, Ethan. . . . I know, I mean, you haven't . . ."

My eyes widen as I realize that she's lumping me in with Sophie. Sophie stabbed Emme in the back by manipulating their supposed friendship for her personal gain. And I . . . well, I've messed up countless times and it seems that Emme hasn't forgotten, or forgiven, my past indiscretions.

You've changed! Remind her of that, don't sit there and let her think the worst of you!

My mouth opens. "It's okay, Emme. You've been through a lot. You have nothing to be sorry for. Nothing."

What the hell? Seriously, dude? You're going to waste this moment! Coward!

She lets out a halfhearted laugh. "Yeah, well, you're probably one of the few people who think that."

Tell her you love her! Say the words! Don't let her go! Don't waste this moment!

"I doubt that."

Idiot!

She gets up and looks at her reflection in the mirror. "Ugh. I'm a mess."

"It's not that bad."

WHAT DID YOU JUST SAY?

"I'm so tired. I just want to go home. . . ."

She turns around and stops herself when she sees me. She studies me for a second. "Are *you* okay, Ethan? You look, um, I don't know. Is everything okay?"

I realize that I've been holding my breath. It probably looks like I'm going to burst. So I say the only thing I can think of.

"No, I'm fine."

God, I loathe you.

Join the club.

EMME

I think I'm having a nervous breakdown.

I get overwhelmed about not only getting to play my song at the Senior Showcase, but getting the last spot, with the band.

Then I'm not even allowed to celebrate it because I basically dress Sophie down in front of the entire school.

So I do what I've been really good at doing lately, which is cry uncontrollably.

And then I insult Ethan.

Clearly, there is something wrong with me.

But Ethan, being Ethan, either doesn't notice it or is too nice to say anything about it.

All I know is that I can't lose another friend. And Ethan, unlike Sophie, is a true friend. I know that he cheats on his girlfriends and does some pretty stupid things, but he's always been there for me.

And I need him more than ever, now that we have to focus on the showcase and college auditions.

Jack bursts through the door with a shopping bag. "Costume time!"

We're playing our last gig of the year and are going to do some Christmas songs, so Jack thought it would be appropriate for us to be as festive as possible. He hands Ethan a Santa jacket, Ben some elf ears, me tinsel, and keeps a Santa hat for himself.

He looks in the mirror. "Man, I make anything look hot!"

We all groan. I start wrapping myself up in the tinsel.

Jack comes over to study me. "You'd make one fine gift under the tree, Red. Don't you think so, Ethan?"

Ethan freezes with his jacket halfway on. "Um, sure?"

"'Um, sure?'" Jack makes a face. "What's wrong with you?"

"I'm trying to figure out why we all have to wear something idiotic and all you have to do is put on a hat?"

Ben takes that as his cue to debate with Jack over why he has to be an elf. There's a knock on the door and I can't believe it when I see who it is.

"Carter!" I run over and give him a hug. "I thought you weren't coming back for two more weeks."

"Change of plans. I didn't want to miss Christmas in New York." He gives me a tight squeeze and then greets everybody in the room.

"Nice ears," he says to Ben.

"That's it!" Ben throws the ears down. "I am *not* going to be the elf."

Ben and Jack start to argue again about the costumes.

Carter comes over to me. "Yikes, didn't realize that was going to set him off."

"It doesn't take much with those two."

Ethan shakes Carter's hand. "Hey, man, did you hear who the spotlight performance for the showcase went to?"

Carter's eyes get wide. "Aw, that's amazing! Congrats, you guys!"

He pats me on the back.

Ethan shakes his head. "No, the band is second to last. It's Emme. Solo."

Carter picks me up. "Emme, I'm so proud of you! Tell me everything."

I go to a corner and sit down with Carter and fill him in on everything that happened with Sophie.

"Ah, gotta love karma. What goes around, comes around," Carter says.

"I guess. . . ." I don't want to think about Sophie anymore. "YOU need to tell me everything! How was Italy?"

Carter gushes, "Amazing. We went to all these art museums and I ate so much pasta. It was a goal Mom and I had — to eat pasta and gelato every day. She's already signed up for some master cleanse the day after Christmas. But we had a lot of fun and I loved that not once did I get recognized. For the first time in my life, nobody cared who I was. My only movies that are shown over there are from when I was really young, so I was just a guy with his mom. I've never had that before."

Carter looks so relaxed and happy. He never really appeared to be miserable, but I think before it was an act and now it's real.

He continues. "So I bought a ton of art books abroad and have been really inspired to paint. I'm going to start working with a tutor to take the GED in a couple months, then art school."

"That's great, Carter. I'm really proud of you."

He nods to himself. "Thanks. Me, too. I can't believe how much things have changed in the last couple of months. Who knows, maybe someday you'll be coming to one of my art openings! Crazier things have happened."

I laugh. Certainly, out of everything that has transpired since the beginning of school, Carter holding an art exhibition would be considered extremely normal.

"Guys!" Jack gets up and starts jumping up and down. "We got five minutes."

Carter excuses himself and the four of us get in a circle.

We put our arms around each other and Jack leans in for what's supposed to be a pep talk, but he usually ends up insulting each of us. "Okay, our last Christmas gig. Ethan's sober, so that's an improvement over last year. . . . Red is going to rock her guitar solo, although try to not make the rest of us look so inferior, O Red One. . . . Ben, you look adorable in your elf ears."

Our hands go into the center.

Jack shouts out, "*Jack rules* on three. One, Two!"

"Jack sucks!" The three of us shout back.

"Aww, come on, where's the love?"

We all walk out to the stage with Jack shouting, "Forget about your presents now!"

There's no way we aren't going to get our presents from Jack.

After the show, the four of us head to Ethan's house, and Jack makes a big to-do about our presents. We each open our gifts to find a framed, near life-size photo of Jack's face.

"I know you guys are going to miss me. . . ." His smile fades at the words.

The rest of us exchange presents. I got each of the guys a personalized leather notebook filled with sheet music.

"For when you get inspired and aren't near a computer."

"You're so old-school, Red!" Jack gives me a kiss on the cheek.

Ethan comes up to me. "Hey, Emme, your gift is on its way. I'm so sorry."

"Don't even worry about it." Ethan always goes a little over the top with gifts. I'm usually embarrassed by my present in comparison, so I'm somewhat grateful that I don't need to feel guilty tonight.

He hands Jack and Ben their presents. Jack unwraps personalized drumsticks with his name and a logo that Trevor designed, while Ben receives designer guitar picks and a matching guitar strap.

"My turn!" Ben hands us each a square box. We untie the bright red and green ribbon to find another notebook. "Look inside."

I open the front cover and gasp. "It's the first picture taken of us." I start flipping through and it is filled with flyers, set lists, ticket stubs of all our concerts.

I don't want to cry . . . again. Especially in front of the guys. I hate to be the stereotype of the girl of the group.

"This is awesome. . . ." I hear Jack's voice crack. "Got something in my eye." He wipes away a tear and gives Ben a big bear hug.

The four of us start reminiscing as we go through the scrapbook. The dives we've played in, the technical difficulties, the *one* groupie . . . I wouldn't take back a single thing.

"Well, ladies . . . and Ethan" — Jack gets up from the couch — "I've got my hot girlfriend waiting for me."

"I'll share a taxi with you." Ben grabs his jacket.

I stand up. "I probably should head out."

"Emme, there's all this cake left." Ethan motions toward the half-eaten chocolate cake on the coffee table.

"Oh, well . . ."

Ethan hands me a fork, and Ben and Jack both hug me good night.

I sit down on the plush carpet and dive into the cake. Ethan knows the way to my heart — not that he's after that; he just knows I like food.

I stare at the gigantic Christmas tree in the corner of the room. The white lights decorating the tree fill the room with a soft white glow.

Ethan goes over to the tree and grabs a huge gift-wrapped rectangle.

"Okay, I lied. I have your gift but didn't want you to open it in front of the guys."

Oh.

He sets down the oversize gift and already I know it's too much. I start to tear away the wrapping, to find a cardboard box with no markings. Ethan leans over to cut the tape around the box with a knife.

I lift the tabs open and dig around the plastic wrapping and pull out a black guitar case.

"Ethan . . ."

I'm scared to open it. It's a guitar. And I'm sure it isn't from Target, like the ones I use.

I unzip the bag to find a candy apple red electric guitar. But not just any electric guitar, a 1964 Fender Stratocaster.

"I can't . . ."

Ethan takes the guitar out and hands it to me.

"I know what you're going to say. But I saw this the other day and thought that you *need* to have it. So consider it a Christmas, Birthday, Graduation, Kicking Ass at the showcase, and Getting into Juilliard gift."

"It's still too much." The guitar is beautiful and I start to strum it. Even unplugged, it sounds wonderful.

"Okay, add putting up with me, holding my hand at the hospital, believing in me, and such."

I shake my head. I know he won't stop until I accept it.

"Plus," he continues, "imagine the damage you can do on your guitar solos with it."

I run my hands up and down the bright red polish. Holding it, I know I won't be able to give it back. I want to plug it in and play.

"And, you know, just remember this gift when we both get into Juilliard."

I look at him and finally get what he means. He always keeps mentioning about what happens if we both get in.

"Ethan, do you think that I wouldn't want you to go to Juilliard?"

He shrugs. "I don't know. I sometimes think that maybe you want to go to school by yourself. . . . Start anew, I guess."

"To be honest, I can't think past the audition. I know you're going to get in, so when I think about Juilliard, I just assume we'll be there together. But if not, I'll be in Boston. Look at me, like I'm just assuming that Berklee will accept me.

"I just need to take things one at a time. First the showcase, then the auditions. You know that I can't handle too many things at once. I've vowed to not turn into a sobbing wreck for the rest of the semester."

It's getting late, so I get up to leave. Then a thought comes to me. "Hey, Ethan? If I wrote accompaniments, do you think you and the guys would join me on my song?"

"You know we'd love to."

It doesn't feel right to not have them up there with me for my song. Plus, I think adding guitars and a drum would make it a lot stronger. I know that I'd be sad when they left the stage, plus it is one of the last performances we'll be doing. I want us to do as much together as possible before we all head our separate ways.

I turn around before I head to the door. "I'm going to really miss the band next year."

"There's always the summer," he suggests.

But we both know that with the four of us spread across the country, it is going to be hard to pick up right where we left off. Sure, we'll probably play together, but it won't be the same. Nothing will be the same.

I look at Ethan and I know he's harder on himself than anybody I've ever known. He's so self-critical, and it doesn't help that Jack teases him all the time, or that I yelled at him. But after The Incident and The Injury, he's been a lot calmer and hasn't exhibited his usual self-destructive behavior.

"I'm really proud of you," I say.

He looks taken aback.

"Really. I know you've been through a lot, probably tortured yourself more than you should. But when I think about next year, it will make me sad if we aren't together. You mean a lot to me. I never would've had the courage to do that solo if it wasn't for you. So I guess I better practice extra hard so I get in."

"You're going to get in."

And the way he says it, it's like it's a fact. A done deal.

But when Ethan says things like that to me, I believe him. Not because I have a bloated self-esteem, but because when he says it, I want to believe it.

I want to be that person he thinks I am.

ETHAN

*A*nd I thought things were bad before.

After winter break, we come back to the Showcase Stress Tsunami. The tension is palpable.

The four of us have a pact that there will be no talk about the upcoming college auditions until after the showcase. We don't even have any gigs to distract us. It is all showcase, all the time.

I'm heading to our practice room when I see a very familiar strand of red hair poking out of a mass of two guitars, one oversize backpack, and a puffy winter coat.

"Emme!" I call out.

She turns around and accidentally drops one of her guitars. I pick it up.

"Here, give me that as well." I take her backpack. "Are you trying to hurt yourself?"

She smiles at me . . . and my heart melts. Every time.

"Can it be May already?" She picks up her other guitar. "I'm not sure if the guitar should be electric or acoustic for my song. . . . I keep changing my mind, so I thought I'd bring both. Although maybe I should play the piano instead?"

"You're not hiding behind the piano on this one."

She bites her lip. "Yeah, but why do you get to?"

"Because it isn't my moment."

She stops walking. "Can we stop referring to the showcase as *my* moment? Anytime I think about it, I get sick to my stomach."

I nod. I'd pretty much agree to anything she says. But it will be her moment.

We enter the room and start unpacking our gear. I reach in my pocket and hand her a protein bar.

She waves it away.

"You've got to eat something."

Her stomach pains have gotten worse with the showcase just a week away. She's hardly been eating and she's thin enough as is. Not like I should talk, but when I'm nervous, I eat more. Which is probably why I've gained so much weight (granted, it was needed) since I've been at CPA. Constant nerves.

After she hooks her guitar up, I guide her to a seat.

She looks up at me like she's waiting for a big lecture. I unwrap the bar and hand it to her. "Please eat something."

She takes a small bite.

Jack bursts into the room with his arm around Ben. "Guess who got their early acceptance to Oberlin today?"

Emme screams. "Ben, that's so fantastic!" She gets up and hugs him.

Jack laughs. "Just think about it. A year from now, I'll be in sunny LA, fighting off the advances of the all-bikini-clad female students at CalArts, while the rest of you will be freezing your butts off, this one in the Midwest and you two albinos here."

Emme takes one more bite of the protein bar. She looks at it for a couple seconds and runs over to a garbage can to spit it out.

"What, Red, are you sick to your stomach over the thought of being so far away from me? I'd say you should come to LA, but I think you'd probably spontaneously combust if you stepped into the sun."

I ignore Jack and run over to Emme.

"Sorry, it tastes like chalk." She hands it back to me. "I'll be fine . . . once, um, the auditions are over. I hope."

She whips out her water bottle and takes a big sip. She turns her attention to Ben. "Ben, you have to tell us everything. What did the letter say? When did you find out?"

Ben hands us a copy of the e-mail he got just a few minutes before. "I had to run to the computer lab to print it out. It seemed like a joke."

"That's really great." I give him a big hug.

I don't know why I haven't been stressing about college acceptance as much as everybody else. I mean, let's face it, I'm never the calm, cool, collected one. I guess I figure that I'll get in somewhere, although I really want to stay in New York and go to

Juilliard with Emme. That's my dream world. Pretty much everything involving Emme and the future is a dream, one that I know won't necessarily come true.

I know I want to write songs and I'll be happy doing it at a prestigious college or for three people at a coffee shop. Not like I don't think I could learn something at Juilliard or any music college; it just isn't as important to me as it is to everybody else.

But seeing the look on Ben's face, I'm thinking that maybe it should be. I've never seen him happier. "Thanks," he says. "It's like this huge weight has been lifted off my shoulders. I don't have to stress about . . ." He stops himself. Because the three of us still have our auditions and fates to worry about. "Well, we still have the showcase. Are we ready?"

We run through my song a few times; it's something we've been playing for a while now. Of course, that doesn't stop me from messing up the lyrics twice, but everybody else sounds great.

After we're all satisfied, our attention turns to Emme's song. I move my mic stand down several inches so the microphone can reach her.

She tentatively approaches the mic and adjusts it for way longer than she needs to. She finally turns around. "Um, okay. I guess we'll start. So I was thinking that it would be best for me to start first." She strums several chords and then nods for the rest of us to join in. We get to the part where she's supposed to start singing and she simply keeps playing the song. "Obviously I'll sing here," she says as she moves closer to the drum kit and farther away from the microphone.

Jack stops drumming. "Red, you've got to own the song and the mic. Go all 'Beat It' on it!"

"I'm embarrassed."

Jack groans. "If you can't sing in front of us, how are you going to do it at the showcase?"

"I don't think I *can* do it." Her voice is barely a whisper.

"Can we take a break?" I ask. Both Jack and Ben leave the room. Emme remains frozen.

I wrap my arm around her. "You can do this."

"I don't know why I agreed to audition in the first place."

"Obviously, the board saw something in you."

She nods for a few minutes. "I'm not used to singing anywhere besides your studio."

"Okay, so close your eyes."

She looks up at me and it kills me that she doesn't trust me enough to just close her eyes.

"Please trust me."

She closes them.

"Okay, pretend that we're in my studio. Sing."

"I feel silly."

"Not as silly as you'll feel if you become a mute onstage."

She feels around her guitar and strums until she finds the first chord. She starts playing and then she opens her mouth. Her lovely voice comes out and floats and twists in the air. Granted, she hasn't had the years of training that the singers in the vocal department have had. So she's not a technically proficient singer. But what makes her special is her soul. She makes the song hers. You don't need to leap ten octaves to do that. You just have to feel it. I'm mesmerized when she sings. I'm only inches away from her while she's lost in her song, breathing every inch of her in.

She finishes and I make her start again. She plays and I do my best to navigate my awkward, gangly body as quietly as possible to get Jack and Ben back in the room. The door makes a tiny squeak, but she doesn't stop. Jack and Ben come in and Jack stops dead in his tracks as he hears her sing. His mouth drops open and mouths, "Oh my Red!"

As she strums the final chord of the song, she smiles and opens her eyes. She looks over and her cheeks grow hot when she sees Ben and Jack.

Jack starts to clap. "Red, is there a reason you haven't been singing all this time? We could've been the band with the hot chick singer. Man. Although there'd be more dudes at the shows, so I guess this is a good thing. Not like the girls that fall over this one are anything to write home about." He winks at me.

I don't blame Jack when he says stuff like that, but I cringe inside that Emme has to hear it.

"Okay, do it one more time, with your eyes open, and we'll just listen, okay?"

She hesitates. "Okay."

By the third run-through, she's comfortable enough that we all join in. I've heard countless songs that Emme has written. But playing along with her, I realize how intricate the chord progressions are, how intimate the lyrics are. It makes me want to go back and read everything she's ever written. It also makes me realize something, and I'm pretty sure I'm not blinded by my infatuation on this one. Everybody has always said that I'm the best songwriter in class and I've always believed it.

Until now.

If I'm counting correctly, we are only halfway through the showcase, and already backstage we've had three people puke, one dancer faint, and one act come off the stage in tears.

What a wonderful way to show off the most talented students at CPA.

My mind starts to race and I get up and start to do jumping jacks. Any physical activity helps distract me. Jack enlisted himself to be the comic relief/distracter to Emme. But I secretly think that Jack's playing the clown to sidetrack himself from the upcoming performance.

I really wanted the job of being with Emme, but I'm so worried that I'd say the wrong thing . . . or that something would go wrong and I'd get blamed for it. So I'm here if she wants me.

The list of upcoming performers starts to dwindle. From backstage we can hear the different songs and performances. It really is inspiring to be part of this, but terrifying to close the show.

We're given the notice that we're next. We head to the wings of the stage. Jack motions for us to get in a circle so he can give us his pep talk.

"So . . ." Jack clears his throat. "We . . ."

Is Jack Coombs at a loss for words? I guess we don't have to worry about the performance since the world is clearly going to end.

"Guys." Emme speaks. "I want to thank you for being there for me, and not just tonight, but the last four years."

There is an understood silence between us. Jack likes to think he speaks for us, but Emme is the one who gets us the most.

Jack sighs. "All this sincerity is starting to freak me out."

Emme laughs. "Fine. Jack, you need to learn to start chewing with your mouth closed."

"That's more like it!"

"Ben, um, I believe your use of hair products is responsible for a significant loss of the ozone layer."

Ben starts laughing. "That is hilarious."

"And so true." Jack reaches up to mess up Ben's perfectly coifed hair, but Ben slaps his hand away before any real damage is done.

"And, Ethan . . ." Emme looks at me with a hint of mischief in her eyes.

Jack starts to clap his hands. "Oh, this one is gonna be good. You can do it, Red!"

"Ethan . . ." She looks up at me. "Ethan . . ."

She hesitates. I'm smiling like I'm waiting for my dis, but I'm really happy that she's having such a hard time thinking of something nasty to say to me. Or she's just being polite because we all know there are plenty of things she can use as ammunition.

"Ethan, you might want to consider more deodorant if you feel the need to do cardio before a performance."

On second thought.

Jack barrels over, laughing. "And the student has become the master."

"We've got this, guys!" Emme beams and I can tell that she means every word.

We get in our places and Emme leans in. "I don't think you smell. I couldn't think of anything to say. You smell nice. . . . I mean, you . . . never mind."

I lean over and give her a kiss on the forehead.

She looks down at the floor and smiles. I move my head to brush my cheek against my shoulder to get a whiff of my pits, just in case.

Dr. Pafford introduces us and we take the stage. The reception is a lot more polite than we receive at gigs or school functions (when family members are obligated to be enthusiastic).

We start my song and everything feels right. After four years, our band is a tight, cohesive unit. At one point I glance at Emme, then turn to Ben, and they both look like they're enjoying themselves.

Come to think of it, I am, too. And I'm sure if I had eyes in the back of my head, I'd see Jack with that intense/happy look he always has at gigs.

What's odd is that the pressure was getting the spot. Not this, this is what we're used to, what we love: performing, being a group.

It's the uncertainty of being accepted that creates the drama in our lives.

My song ends and I head to the piano as Emme adjusts the microphone.

I look at her and know exactly what she's going through. Although I only had to face a group of about twenty people at our first gig. She is looking out toward hundreds of administrators, talent scouts, and prestigious alumni.

But for me, these guys having my back gave me the courage to do it. I don't know if I'll ever have the desire to be a "front man" again without them behind me.

Emme glances at me and gives me a little nod as she starts playing her song. We all join in and I can hardly breathe as we approach the first verse.

She sings the first line and her voice is quivering and soft. A knot forms in my stomach. The next line is louder, but the shaking comes through a lot stronger.

You can do this, Emme. Please believe that you can do it. Please, Emme.

There is a four-bar break and she steps away from the mic and I see her nodding now, trying to get into the song. If I could stop the song to give her a pep talk, I would. But it's all in her hands now.

She approaches the microphone again for the second verse. She opens her mouth and a loud, clear voice comes out. I see some people sit up a little straighter in the audience.

I smile as I close my eyes and take in her voice. She's got this. I try to concentrate on the chords, but I'm absolutely spellbound by her. I let the hours of practice take over, and go into automatic mode so I can witness her transformation to the lead.

The instrumental break comes and she turns around to us and she's beaming. She smiles at me and my heart nearly bursts.

She sings the chorus once more and then the last note hangs in the air.

We get applause, greater than we did when we arrived onstage, but not the rousing ovation we've gotten in the past. This crowd is a little tougher.

Plus, we are performing for the possibilities of building our futures. Not to entertain our grandparents.

The four of us take center stage, link hands, and bow.

As we head offstage, I notice that Emme still has my hand . . . but she also has Jack's.

As soon as we get offstage, Emme whispers to me, "I botched the first verse."

"But you killed the rest of the song," I assure her.

She squeezes my hand. "You were really great."

I see Jack walk away to get a hug from Chloe. Emme's hand is still in mine.

"So were you. I didn't know you had such a big voice."

She blushes. "Oh, well, I figured I had to do something, so I went with loud."

"It suits Jack well."

She laughs. Then looks down and it seems like it's the first time she's noticing that she's holding my hand.

"Oh, sorry." She lets go.

I want to grab it back from her. I want to grab *her*. But I don't. I can be a complete idiot at times, but I like to think that I've learned from the mistake of attacking her after the "Beat It" performance.

Instead I sit there silently as I watch her get approached by other students.

I hear a few words of congratulations thrown my way, but I don't feel like celebrating.

I envisioned being done with the showcase as this momentous occasion. We'd get a standing ovation and the four of us would leave the stage and get in a group huddle. Tell each other how incredible we were and block out the rest of the world. Then when we broke up the huddle, Emme would look at me and realize how much I mean to her. I'd confess my love for her, she'd realize her true feelings for me, and we'd be together.

But instead, we're all separated, talking to other people.

The showcase is over, my life is the same.

Nothing is going to change her feelings.

In a few short months, this part of my life will be done. We'll all be going our separate ways.

I'm an idiot for thinking that one performance would change anything.

Maybe I should stop writing songs and start writing fiction.

EMME

I can't find Ethan anywhere. I've been searching the post-showcase reception and he's nowhere to be found.

Last time he disappeared, he ended up in the hospital. I get out my phone to text him, when I'm approached by a balding man in a suit.

"Excuse me, young lady, you were tremendous." He hands me his business card. "I oversee a performing arts summer camp for ages eight and up. We're looking for counselors to do music programs."

"Oh, thanks." He pats me on the back before he approaches Trevor with his card out.

I text Ethan and hear Mr. North call out my name. He comes over and shakes my hand. "That was fantastic. How are you feeling?"

"Good."

"Making any connections?"

I shake my head. "Do you know who the Juilliard and Berklee representatives are?"

"They don't come to the reception. All the heavy hitters have left. These are people usually looking for interns, summer help, free food . . ."

"Dan!" A woman in a gray suit calls out to Mr. North.

"And the alumni who want to relive their glory years. Duty calls. . . ."

He heads toward the woman, and Tyler approaches me.

"You were really great tonight." He gives me a quick hug.

"Thanks, so were you."

He shrugs. "Well, Sarah and I have been practicing for months on the song. So . . ."

We both nod and I don't think it could be any more awkward. I want to tell him that I like him, that I'm sorry things have been crazy, but truthfully, things are going to get even worse now that college auditions are next.

I get a text on my phone and it's from Ethan.

"Oh, I, um . . ."

Tyler sees my screen. "No, of course. I think I need to work this room more than you anyway. Have a good one." He walks away from me, and I stay frozen for a few seconds. I take one more look around the reception before I head out.

Ethan is sitting on the steps outside.

"Hey."

He looks up at me. "Hey."

I sit down next to him. "It's a little cold out. . . ."

He nods.

I can tell there is something wrong with him, but I have no idea what. He did amazing tonight; he always does. He can be too critical of his performance, but I was getting the feeling he didn't really care too much about the showcase.

"Well, tonight's been a letdown," I say to him.

He looks at me with a weird expression.

"What?" I ask.

He shakes his head. "Nothing. It's just I feel the exact same way."

"Sort of anticlimactic, huh?"

"Yeah, they've built up the showcase since freshman year and it's done. And . . ." He lets his last word hang in the air.

"I thought we'd be swarmed by all these admissions people from Juilliard or the Manhattan School of Music. All I have is a pocket full of business cards with offers to teach music lessons. Which is a compliment, but still . . ."

He doesn't respond.

"You know what I can't help thinking about?" He stays silent. "These seashells that Sophie gives me . . . I guess *used to* give me every summer. Maybe we've been making too much out of the showcase because really our journey isn't done yet. We've been focusing so much on getting there that we haven't been enjoying the ride."

I'm not sure I'm making any sense.

"I forget who said it, but it was something like 'focus on the journey, not the destination.' You know what I'm going to remember most about CPA? It's not the showcase, it's being with you guys, our rehearsals, Jack's crazy tales of our ultimate demises — everything."

Ethan nods. "Yeah, I guess you're right. We've all been chasing something that isn't really there. At least I know I have."

I don't really know what to say. Ethan can be overly reflective at times, and now he seems somber, like he's lost something. But we had a great evening. So we don't have recruiters banging down our doors, but we do have something to celebrate.

I get up and hold out my hand. He stares at it and doesn't move.

His reaction is depressing me even more. I'm so exhausted I want to just curl up in a ball and sleep for a year. But I can't let this evening end like this.

"Ethan, it's freezing out. Let's get out of here. I'll text Ben and Jack, and we can celebrate the fact that we not only survived the showcase, we rocked it. Come on, my treat! You know I couldn't have done any of that if it wasn't for you guys."

He gets up, but doesn't take my hand. He walks ahead of me and doesn't speak the entire walk to the diner. Ben, Jack, and Chloe meet up with us, and none of us talk about the showcase. Because all along we assumed that was our challenge. That all the stress would disappear once it was over.

But it is only the beginning.

Our college auditions.

And we each have to go it alone.

CARTER

here hasn't been a single moment that I've regretted walking out of CPA's doors. I'll admit that the headline CARTER HARRISON: HIGH SCHOOL DROPOUT made me cringe, but taking those weeks off with my mom in Italy was exactly what I needed. I was relaxed, I was inspired, I was plain old Carter.

But the vacation is over. I thought I'd come back and finally be able to support Emme for once as she gets ready for her college auditions. But she's been in lockdown rehearsing and I've found that trying to accomplish years of work in a few months is a lot harder than I ever imagined it would be.

I'm watching my tutor look through my practice GED test. She keeps marking things up and nodding her head.

TUTOR: Okay, it's not awful.

Well, that's just fabulous news.

TUTOR: You did really well on the language arts
sections, both the writing and reading. I guess all
those years of reading scripts have paid off. What
you're having problems with is the math section,
particularly with the algebra questions. You
technically passed the math section, but we need to
get that number up higher so your overall percentage
doesn't suffer.

She pulls out these bulky math workbooks from her bag,
flips through the thin pages, and begins to mark sections with
Post-it notes.

TUTOR: I want you to work on these five sections for
our next meeting.

I look at the hundreds of algebra problems facing me in the
next three days.

And here I thought I'd figured out the equation to my
happiness.

I start going through the problems as my mom shows
her out.

MOM: Do you want to get an algebra-specific tutor?

I shake my head.

MOM: You know you can take your time; you don't have to take the exam right away.

ME: I know, but I want this to be over so I can move on to art school.

Mom sits down and pinches the upper bridge of her nose. I've only seen her do that a few times. The last time was when I was no longer a Kavalier Kid. That seems like a lifetime ago . . . probably because it was.

MOM: Honey, I've been doing some research and I think you're going to have to wait until next year to apply. Most schools aren't accepting any more applications for fall.

ME: I know.

MOM: Oh.

My mind races as to what to say. I've spent so much of my life hiding my feelings, it's been harder than I thought to open up and not keep things a secret any longer. I know I don't have to do this alone. I know that Mom is trying to help me.

And I know that I've got to get over it already.

ME: Yeah, sorry, Mom. I realized that when I saw I missed National Portfolio Day.

Mom looks at me blankly.

ME: Yeah, it's this really cool thing I found online. It's a day where representatives from colleges all over the country meet with prospective students and review their portfolios. It's supposed to help you get a stronger portfolio for colleges. They take place in the fall, so I figured, if it's okay with you, that I'd spend the next year taking some basic classes and get a portfolio ready for next year. I'm kinda behind as is and need the catch-up time.

Mom smiles as me. She gets up from the table and hugs me.

MOM: Of course. You've been working your entire life. You deserve to have a break.

I don't know how much of a break it's going to be. I'm going to be competing against people who've been studying art their whole lives. I might not have what it takes, but I've at least got to try. I owe myself that much.

★   ★   ★   ★   ★   ★   ★   ★   ★   ★   ★   ★   ★   ★

How many times have I sat in a hallway waiting for my name to be called?

But this is entirely different. My legs shake as I sit in the office of the Museum of Modern Art in Manhattan. I've never had anybody but my mom and my friends look at my art. I've never had anybody critique my work who *knew* what they were talking about — someone who wasn't required to praise me out of the unspoken rule that you support your son or friend no matter how bad they may suck at something.

This is a stupid idea. Why on earth didn't I go to some community art school to hear what a teacher thinks of me? Why am I about ready to enter the offices of one of the top art museums in the world to get a curator's opinion? I know it's something most artists could only dream of, and it's because of who I am, and a favor from Sheila Marie, that's gotten me in the door.

I'm shocked I don't jump out of my skin when my name is called.

I follow a young woman in a suit down a narrow hallway. Her heels make a clicking noise as I follow her and realize that my heart is pounding in unison. She gestures to me to enter an office, and Mr. Samuels gets up from his pristine desk.

MR. SAMUELS: Mr. Harrison, so glad to meet you.

ME: Thank you so much for having me here. I don't want to take too much of your time.

I thought I was done with acting, but I'll need to take out everything in my bag of tricks to pretend that I'm not terrified at this very moment. I think back to the first time I was interviewed on a live morning show when I was eight. I had to get up at five in the morning to make it to the studio in time for hair and makeup. (Yep, even an eight-year-old boy needs hair and makeup early in the morning.) I remember Mom told me to smile although I was terrified. She said it would fool my brain into thinking that I was happy and relaxed.

I wonder what Mr. Samuels must be thinking of the stupid grin on my face now.

> MR. SAMUELS: I don't know if Sheila Marie told you, but my daughter is a huge fan of your *Kavalier Kids* movies. I can't tell you how many times we watched the first movie during the summer last year.

Mr. Samuels picks up a framed photo from his desk and hands it to me. He continues to talk about his daughter and family while I politely study the smiling face of a ten-year-old girl.

> MR. SAMUELS: Listen to me going on and on. What can I do for you today? I see you brought your portfolio.

> ME: Yes.

My voice cracks. I cough a couple times to recover.

ME: Sorry, yes. I'm hoping to apply to art schools next
year, but I haven't had any formal training. I'm going
to take some basic classes starting this summer, but
since I haven't really been critiqued by anybody, I just
needed to know . . .

The words scare me. The thought of what I could hear
frightens me.

ME: I just need to know if I have any promise at all. If
there is any hope for me. And I really am looking for
an honest opinion, Mr. Samuels. I understand that my
art is going to be amateurish at best compared to
what you see on a daily basis.

I motion toward the framed posters lining his office walls, of
different exhibitions he's curated.

ME: I'm sure you can imagine that I've had a lot of
people sugarcoat things for me because of who I am.
But none of that has helped me, so I'd really like to
hear what you think of my art, where I need to
improve . . . and if there is anything here that could
possibly get me into an art school.

Mr. Samuels nods his head and unzips my portfolio. One by one he lays out my sketches and paintings on his desk and examines each piece. I decided to give him a mix of what I've been working on: pencil and charcoal drawings, paintings in different styles. But mostly the portfolio is filled with my sketches. Since I kept my passion for art a secret, I didn't have the courage to really set up a painting studio until a few months ago.

Mr. Samuels places several of the paintings against a wall and steps back and examines them for what seems like an eternity. I can't read the reaction on his face and try to not stare. The last thing I want is the man who is basically going to validate the biggest decision of my life to feel self-conscious. After all, he's not the one being judged.

You'd think I'd be used to that by now, but in the past, I didn't care about my acting. So the opinions didn't matter as much as this one.

I decide to fold my shaking hands, willing them to be still. I notice a fleck of red paint on my wrist and start picking at it.

After what seems like forever (but is probably only ten minutes . . . ten long, agonizing minutes), Mr. Samuels sits down and takes off his glasses.

MR. SAMUELS: You wanted honest, correct? Because there is good news and there's bad, but not uncorrectable, news.

A lump rises in my throat. What if the good news is that I can always fall back on my acting?

ME: That's exactly what I was hoping for, sir.

He picks up two of my black-and-white charcoal sketches: one I did of Emme playing the piano and another of my mother reading.

MR. SAMUELS: Your use of light and shadow is
impressive.

He traces the curve of Emme's neck down to her hands. I remember that day because the sun was hitting the practice suite and illuminated one side of her, while the other was cast in a dark shadow.

Mr. Samuels grabbed another sketch I did in Central Park at night, right before a thunderstorm.

MR. SAMUELS: And the mood of this piece is
especially foreboding and mature for someone
your age.

My spirits start to lift. But I steady myself because I'm waiting for the "but" I know is coming. I've also noticed that he put my paintings and color sketches off to one side.

He looks up from the paintings and smiles at me.
But . . .

MR. SAMUELS: Tell me, Carter, how long have you
been working with paint?

And here it comes.

ME: I've really only been working with acrylics for
the last six months or so.

He nods.

MR. SAMUELS: I can see that you don't have much
control over the brush yet. That's something that
comes with time, so you might want to start off by
taking some introductory painting classes. But my
real concern is your lack of identity.

Tell me about it.
He lays out four of my paintings.

MR. SAMUELS: We've got two abstract paintings,
realism, and pointillism. Different styles by the same
artist. While I'm seeing a lot of versatility — and don't
get me wrong, that can be a good thing — there's no
consistency. Something that tells me I'm looking at

something by *you*. I don't really see *you* in these pieces. What kind of statement do *you* want to make with your art? What is it that *you* are trying to tell us?

I guess that has been the real question all along.

MR. SAMUELS: While you can learn about proper brush technique and color theory, you can't be schooled in what makes you want to create. Some artists spend their entire lives searching for their identity, so don't let this discourage you. Because there is talent in here, true talent. And that, Mr. Harrison, can't be taught at even the best schools.

I feel myself exhale. Mr. Samuels continues to give me advice and I automatically write down notes, but one thought goes through my mind: *I am, once and for all, on the right track.*

I've been staring at different blue paints for so long, they all look the same. After my meeting with Mr. Samuels, I felt inspired. It wasn't that I didn't have enough to work on, but that I had some promise. That's all I was looking for. A chance that I could possibly get into art school.

I look over the acrylic section at my favorite art supply store. I want to get right to work on painting more.

A familiar voice calls out my name. I turn around and see the last person I thought I'd see here.

ME: Sophie?

She approaches me and looks tired. I haven't seen her since our breakup and everything that went down between her and Emme.

SOPHIE: Hey, I guess I'd ask you what you're doing here, but . . .

She gestures at my basket full of acrylic paint and brushes.

SOPHIE: I'm just picking up some supplies for a costume I'm making for an audition.

She holds up a bag with sequined stars.

SOPHIE: It's for an off-Broadway show. I've pretty much given up on CPA stuff. I can't wait for graduation.

I nod at her. I guess after all this time, we still have something in common.

ME: Well, good luck. I guess . . .

My mind races for something more to say to her, someone who was a huge part of my life, but I come up with nothing.

SOPHIE: Yeah, thanks . . .

She turns around and hesitates. For a moment, I'm unsure if she's going to run for the exit or do an impromptu concert like she did at one of the store openings we went to when we first dated. She turns back on her heels and faces me.

SOPHIE: I just need to know . . . How could you throw it all away?

ME: Sophie, things weren't working out with us.

SOPHIE: I'm not talking about us.

ME: Well, things weren't working out between me and CPA either.

She shakes her head.

SOPHIE: Not that, your career. You had everything. Most people would kill to be in your position. The money, the fame . . . And you turn your back on it. I don't understand. Do you not have any clue how incredibly lucky you were?

I take a moment to process everything she's said. I guess from the outside, my life seems storybook to some (at least those who think hitting your peak at ten is enviable). But Sophie should know better — she's seen the hours I've had to work, how invasive the press can be. And, yes, I've been lucky. Incredibly lucky. But that and some hard work were all that I had. Not talent. Not passion.

And suddenly it dawns on me. Sophie has had success at CPA even though she doesn't think she has. She's been part of every production. Granted, most of the time it was as a background player, but she still got in. But she was never happy unless she was a star. I think of Emme happily strumming in the background.

ME: Sophie, did I ever tell you about the background artist I became friends with on the *Kids* set?

She stares at me blankly.

ME: He was this really great guy named Bill. He came in every day, sat with the other extras, and never complained. Extras hardly get paid, they don't get any glamour, not to mention lines. They work long hours for no glory. But Bill always had a smile on his face.

I can tell Sophie is getting bored. But I don't care; I think this could help her.

ME: So one day, I went up to him because I wanted to know his story. I found out that he works at a grocery store to help pay the bills, but he'd always loved movies as a kid. So his dream was to spend time on a movie set. He didn't look at the work as being beneath him; he was happy just to be there.

SOPHIE: So what, he turned out to be some famous actor? Or are you saying that I need to think that being stuck in a chorus isn't beneath me?

ME: I'm just saying that if all you want out of a career is money and fame, you're never going to be happy. Not once did you ever show any interest in the ins and outs of my job — you were only interested in the spotlight. You're only happy if you're getting attention, but you aren't going to start at the top. Very few make it, and I'm proof that it doesn't last long. But if you're going to spend your whole life chasing fame, you're going to be a very unhappy person. With everything I've been through, I've learned this one thing: Fame and money aren't worth it if you have nothing else in your life.

I turn my back on her and head for the register. Maybe it's easy for me to tell others that money doesn't matter. I have plenty of it, but I know that no matter what my financial situation was, I'd paint. Even if I was living in a dirty studio apartment and eating instant soup, I'd paint.

Because that's what makes me happy. And I deserve to be happy. Everybody does, even Sophie. But it's up to each of us to find our own way.

I feel like Dr. Jekyll and Mr. Hyde. I spend my mornings studying language arts, social studies, and science. The afternoon, I tackle math. But at night, I paint.

I think all the studying has freed up my painting, and the meeting with Mr. Samuels has given me the confidence to know that I'm moving in the right direction. I'm no longer fixed on getting everything "right" or being precise. I guess spending all day staring at textbooks has, in a weird way, made me looser.

I think of all the personas I've had: Child Actor, Washed-Up Child Actor, Teen Semi-Heartthrob, High School Student. . . . But with the paintbrush in my hand and my mind clear, for the first time I feel like Carter Harrison: Artist. And that fact doesn't embarrass or scare me.

The red paint I've dipped my brush in starts to drip and I let some of the paint go on the canvas. I'm not sure what direction this painting is going, but it's kind of like my life right now.

A work in progress.

And the possibilities are endless.

EMME

*A*fter weeks — okay, months, maybe even years —
of practicing, it's finally time.

My Berklee audition is first. I'm somewhat
grateful since Berklee has an acceptance rate of thirty-five percent, compared to Juilliard's eight percent. Like either of those
odds are in anybody's favor.

I decided to do the audition in New York instead of heading
up to the Boston campus. While I'm used to sitting in the hallway, waiting for my name to be called out, the nerves are
stronger than anything that I experienced at CPA.

I think about how much easier it would be if the guys
were here.

I think about Ben, who doesn't have to deal with auditions
anymore.

I think about Jack, who is auditioning for CalArts today.

I think about Ethan, who had his Berklee audition yesterday.

I think about Carter, who is spending the weekend taking the GED.

What I don't want to think about is next weekend. Doing this all over again, but at Juilliard. And then doing it again for Boston Conservatory, the Manhattan School of Music, and the San Francisco Conservatory.

Fortunately, most of the schools I applied to were part of the Unified Application for Music and Performing Arts Schools, so I only had to do one application for them. But there are auditions for each one.

Maybe by the end, I'll no longer get nervous.

"Emme Connelly."

My name is called out and the taste of bile stings my throat.

Or not.

The school week flies by. I don't think about anything but the Juilliard audition. My audition is a little over two hours after Ethan's. We go to a café near Lincoln Center for breakfast, but I can't eat. Every time I try to put something in my stomach, it either comes back up or tastes like dust.

I annoy the waitress by asking for my eighth glass of water. I push my plate of eggs toward Ethan and he dives in. I wish I could be as confident as him, shoveling in food like he doesn't have a care in the world.

"Thanks for coming early for me," he says as he scrapes the plate clean.

"Thanks for staying late for me."

We go to Juilliard and check in. We get our information packet and head to the practice rooms. We both go over our songs until it's Ethan's turn.

He looks at me expectantly. "Good luck. I know you don't need it, but you're going to be fabulous." I give him a hug and he holds me tight. Maybe he's a little nervous. I'm sure he's been hiding it because if I knew he was nervous, I'd be even more of a wreck.

It feels like he's been gone an eternity. I play through my songs so much that my hands are starting to get sore.

Finally, he opens the door. "How did it go?" I ask, throwing my arms around him. I think I need the hug more than he does.

"Good. The songs were the songs. I don't know how I did during the interview portion — you know I'm not that good with stuff like that."

Ethan can charm any audience. We once had an unruly crowd when we were opening for a metal band. These big, intimidating guys were not fans of ours. But Ethan gave as good as we got, and by the time the featured band was on, the guys were buying Ethan shots. He was fifteen.

We spend the time before my audition going over the interview questions. I've already practiced my answers on Ethan, who would never criticize me, so I don't know if the answers are as good as he says.

All I know is that when my name is called out, my body goes numb. I say something to Ethan, but spend all my energy focusing on walking to the piano onstage.

"This is Emme Connelly and she is applying to the composition program," a man in the audience says over the microphone. I decide to not look at the panel sitting in the audience. I look straight ahead, but something catches my eye. I look over to the side of the stage and see Ethan's head barely poking out. I quickly glance at the panel and they don't see him. But I can.

"Miss Connelly, can you tell us about the first song you will be performing for us?"

Ethan smiles at me and nods for me to continue.

"Yes, it is called 'Defying Chance,' and it's a recent song I wrote about the chances we take in life . . . and how sometimes you've got to forget about chances and believe in yourself."

"Okay, please begin when you are ready."

I take a deep breath but quickly glance at Ethan, who's beaming at me. I play the introduction and start to sing. I keep my eyes closed the entire time, only opening them up every once in a while to steal a look at Ethan.

I play the guitar for my second song, wanting to showcase my versatility with instruments. I can't see Ethan, since I have to face the panel. But I can sense that he's here with me.

I'm relieved only for a moment after my song ends, because now it's my interview time.

"Can you tell us why you wish to get a degree in composition?"

"Yes. Ever since I can remember, I've had a special connection to music. I would spend hours listening to the radio or watching concerts on TV. When I started to take piano lessons, my teacher would get annoyed with me because I'd change the melodies of songs since I wanted them to sound like songs that I had in my head. For so long I thought it was a bad thing to do because I'd always get in trouble. She'd tell me, 'That's not what's written on the page.' I was getting so upset because I wanted to do my own songs, but then when I was six, I got a new teacher who encouraged me to write my own music.

"I love starting with a blank piece of paper and making a new song from scratch. There are many times when I step away from the end of a long day of composing and I'm surprised about how much I did. Like it was coming from someplace else. All I know is that I have this need to create music. And if I don't get into any music programs, I'm still going to do it for as long as I breathe."

I resist the urge to bite my lip. I wish I hadn't said anything about not getting into school like it wouldn't be a big deal. But it's the truth. If I don't make it to a music program, I'll reapply next year to schools for education or business. But music will always be a part of who I am.

"Favorite composers?"

"Mozart, Beethoven, Bach, Rachmaninoff, Gershwin, Lennon/ McCartney."

There is some laughter at the last comment. But I write mostly pop/rock songs, so I'd be an idiot if I omitted probably the biggest musical influence of the past few decades.

"Can you tell us about a challenge you've had to face and how you've grown from it?"

Besides this audition?

"To be honest, being here, onstage, is a challenge. I've never been the kind of person who has a desire to be in the spotlight. What inspires me is the writing, not necessarily performing in front of an audience. Most of the music students I know enjoy seeing their name in lights and being onstage. But that's always been my least favorite part. So standing up here having to sing for you, to have the confidence it requires to be an entertainer, that's been a real challenge.

"However, this experience has really taught me a lot about myself. It's wonderful to have people believe in you, but if you don't believe in yourself, you really can't accomplish much. So the fact that I'm standing here, and I'll be able to walk out that door and be proud of what I've done, is an unbelievable accomplishment. It makes we wonder what else I'm capable of."

I begin to feel a sting come from behind my eyes. I will not cry during my Juilliard audition. I meant every word of what I said. I'm really proud of myself. Every time I thought I would fall on my face, I rose to the occasion. And for the first time, I actually believe that I belong here.

"Why Juilliard?"

"Because it's Juilliard," I blurt out. Apparently I've become too comfortable onstage. . . .

More laughter comes from below.

I try to recover. "I'm from Brooklyn. New York City is part of who I am. I attend the New York City High School of the Creative and Performing Arts, mainly because of its proximity to Juilliard. This has been my dream for so long, I think it would be more difficult for me to answer 'Why would anybody choose *not* to go to Juilliard?' "

There is some whispering among the judges.

"Thank you."

I'm startled. It's over? That's all they're asking me? This is not a good sign. They talked to Ethan for nearly twenty minutes. I got maybe five.

"Thank you so much for your time," I say before I head back to the hallway.

I open the door and see Ethan waiting for me.

He envelops me in his arms. "You were wonderful, the best I've ever heard you."

"Thanks. How did you sneak in?"

"I've got my ways. . . ."

"Did you hear my interview?"

He shakes his head. "I didn't want to get caught, so I left once you couldn't see me anymore."

"They only asked me four questions."

For a second, a look of worry crosses Ethan's face, but he quickly disguises it.

"Emme, I think they only have those interviews to make sure you can string a few words together. Please don't let this ruin the day. We are finished with our auditions. Flippin' Juilliard!"

He's right. It's over. There's nothing I can do now. The chances of me getting in are ... well, eight percent. But I had the opportunity. I've got my other schools, I've got the guys. All will be well.

I hear a rumbling coming from my stomach.

"I'm starving."

Ethan puts his arm around me and leads me out of the building. "It's about time. Let's get some food in you."

I may have annoyed the waitress this morning with my repeated refills of water, but the older gentleman who is waiting on us at the Italian restaurant seems impressed by the amount of food I just packed away.

"Such a skinny girl. You eat more?"

"I think I'm done." I push away my empty plate of chicken parm (which joined my empty plates of bruschetta, mozzarella sticks, and penne alla vodka).

Ethan smiles at me. "That was impressive."

"Ugh. I'm so full. Why did you let me keep ordering?"

"Because you haven't eaten a full meal in weeks."

I rub my belly. "Can we walk through the park? I need to digest this food."

"I think we'd have to walk around the entire isle of Manhattan for that."

I throw my napkin at him. We get up and head east to Central Park. I wrap my scarf around me since all the blood has rushed to my stomach.

We head to the Imagine mosaic near Strawberry Fields. Ethan reassures me for the third time that my Lennon/McCartney answer was good.

"Thanks."

"Of course."

I look over at Ethan and realize that he's been there with me through everything. He's gone above and beyond more times than I deserve. I haven't even missed Sophie at all, because once she went away, I realized that she didn't ever really have an impact on me as a friend. Because she wasn't a friend. Not like Ethan.

I study the Imagine mosaic. The small white and black stones together form a beautiful tribute to one of the greatest songwriters of all time. I see Ethan looking down as well. He's a huge part of my life. If my world was a mosaic, Ethan would be one of the most significant pieces in it.

"Ethan." He looks at me. "I know I say this a lot, but thank you. Truly *thank you*." I feel a lump in my throat. "You have been so kind and generous to me since the day we met. I hope you know that I realize how much you do for me. You really mean the world to me. Seeing you there today made everything better. I couldn't have done this, or a lot of things, without you."

Ethan's leg has been shaking since I began talking. He crosses his arms and takes a deep breath.

"Ethan? Are you okay?"

He looks at me with a serious look that I've never seen before.

"I have to tell you something."

I don't know if it is the food I ate, but I feel sick to my stomach. I'm not sure I can handle Ethan making another confession to me about girls or drinking or even worse. I, more than anything, want to believe that he's stopped with his self-destructive antics.

"Emme, I am deeply and madly in love with you."

ETHAN

 finally find the courage to say the words that have been stuck in my throat for four years. And once they're out there, I realize that I can't stop. I don't want to stop.

"From the moment I saw you on our first day, I thought you were the most beautiful living creature that has ever graced this planet. When you came up to me in the cafeteria, I couldn't believe that you would even speak to me. And every single second since, I have been in shock to have the fortune for you to be in my life.

"I never in a million years could ever think that you would see me as anything but the nerdy songwriter, so I've never said anything to you. I really cared about Kelsey, but she was a consolation prize because I couldn't have you. And I know that sounds cruel, but it's true. And all those girls at the show . . . I wanted you to see that some people found me attractive so that maybe you'd see me a different way. But I knew I was just making things worse. I knew you were so disappointed in me when I messed up. But part of me thought that if I kept messing up, it would give me a reason that you wouldn't be with me. Not that I would ever have a chance. But then after you yelled at me, I had this feeling that you cared about me and, if you could be so passionate about me being an idiot, that if I could be a better person and not try to sabotage everything good in my life, you could see I'm just a guy who wants to do nothing but be in your presence.

"I don't want to ruin our friendship and what we have, but I cannot for another minute stand in front of you without you knowing exactly how I feel. Because I can't see past you. You are everything to me."

I pause for a second. I try to swallow back some of the words. Emme's eyes are wide. I have no idea what is going through her mind. But I need to tell her. I know that if I had to keep this charade up any longer, I would go mad.

I decide to go for broke. "Do you think you can trust me that I've changed, that I can be the person you need in your life and be with me? Emme?"

She blinks a few times and I feel dizzy when I see her bite her lip.

"Ethan . . . I didn't know. . . ."

"You had to know that I am crazy about you. Everybody knows."

She shakes her head. "I didn't think in such a . . . I guess . . ."

She goes over to a bench to sit down. I follow her and kneel so she has no choice but to look me in the eye.

"Ethan, I can't imagine my life without you, but I think . . . I think . . . we should just be friends."

I feel an ache in my chest at the sound of that word. *Friend* is the worst word you can hear when professing your love to someone. I guess if the only way I can have Emme is as a friend, I'll have to settle for it. But I'm lying to myself if I think I can do that. And I'm so used to lying to myself, I know when I'm completely full of it. There's no way I can do that.

A tear starts rolling down her face. "You know that if we were ever together, that if something went wrong, it would ruin the band, it would ruin what we have."

"Or it can make it even better, even more amazing."

"I'm sorry, but I can't."

"Why?" I need to hear her say it. Whatever it is that is stopping her from being with me. Even if it's that she finds me physically repulsive. I need to know, no matter how hard it hurts.

She lifts her head and looks me right in the eyes. "Because it would destroy me if you ever cheated on me. I could never handle that kind of betrayal from you."

It feels as if the wind has been knocked out of me. Emme thinks that I would cheat on her. Because I cheated on Kelsey. A few times. In front of Emme.

"I would never do that to you. I have never betrayed you."

Her shoulders begin to shake as I try to think of what else I could do. I've regretted a lot in my past, but never anything having to do with her, even now when my heart is being ripped in two.

She stands up. "I'm sorry, Ethan. I can't." She won't even look at me before she runs away toward the street.

I stand there frozen until a pain surges in my forehead. I want to scream, I want to bash my head in, I want to shake Emme. No one will ever care for her as much as I do. Never. I need her to see that.

I shake my head, trying to clear the chaos of thoughts erupting in my mind.

There's only one thing I know to do. One thing I can do to get a temporary reprieve from the misery I'm in.

I start to run home.

It takes me less than fifteen minutes to get home, and before I even get there, I already have the first two verses written.

I guess I was kidding myself when I thought that she'd come around. I only got a couple texts from Emme asking if I was okay and saying that she's so sorry.

She's basically apologizing for not loving me.

Yeah, I'm really sorry, too.

I start packing up my bag to head home. Emme and I haven't really spoken since Saturday. Jack and Ben are more than aware that there's something going on. When Jack made a joke about the tension during lunch on Monday, Emme started to cry and left the table. I think I've spoken about five words all week. And those would be "Just leave it alone, Jack."

But we have a gig tonight and it's hard to hide from each other in the tiny room backstage.

I dread even the thought of being in any room — big or small — having to look at Emme and pretend that my life hasn't been shattered into a million little pieces. I force the school's main door open with so much anger that the windows shake.

"Ethan?" I look over to see Carter reading a book on the steps. "Are you okay?"

He gets up.

"What are you doing here?" I don't even pretend to be polite. Not that Carter did anything, but I'm so mad right now, I'd take it out on a blind nun.

"I'm meeting Emme. . . ." He stops himself. His head cocks to the side as if he gets what's going on. "You know this is hard on her, too."

I hate how he can read people like we are all some open book here for his amusement.

"She's not the one who is being rejected." I fold my arms and glare at him.

"It's not that simple."

I start to walk away. What does Carter Harrison know about anything? And I guess he's officially replacing me now? He's Emme's new confidant. I wonder if they're anything else.

My body jerks as Carter grabs my arm. It takes every ounce of self-control to not punch him. "What do you want?"

He returns the hard stare. "Ethan, have you put yourself in Emme's shoes? I don't think she's gotten over how betrayed she was by Sophie. Her best friend for nearly ten years turns out to be a fake who calls her out in front of the entire school. You, Ben, and Jack have been there for her since the beginning of freshman year. Do you have any idea of how scared she is of being hurt again, especially by someone who means as much to her as you?"

"I'd never hurt Emme. I've told her that, but she doesn't believe me. She doesn't want to hear it."

"Then do something to make her hear you."

He drops his grip and walks away.

It pains me to say it, but Carter is right.

I know what I need to do. It's not like I've never done it before. But this time it's different. Because I can't lose the best thing that's ever happened to me.

It's like old times up onstage with the group. And it's not that nostalgic feeling you have when reminiscing about the past.

No, I've become a mute between songs. I do my best to engage the crowd, but I can't focus on them. I've only got one goal before me and it has nothing to do with the mass of people standing in front of me.

I've caught Ben and Emme exchanging knowing looks

during the set. They know something is wrong. But neither one of them has any idea how wrong it all is.

We end with "Beat It," since that's become our signature song. The four of us take a bow and the others start to walk away. But I don't move.

I see Emme pause for a second as she steps offstage. But I start to tune my guitar and try not to wuss out.

Because I'm about ready to do the biggest audition of my life.

"Thanks, everybody." The crowd quiets down. "I'm actually going to do one more number, if that's okay with you." They scream. I block out the movement coming from the side of the stage.

I strum the first few chords of the song. "This is a song I wrote this past weekend, and the guys haven't had a chance to hear it yet." More applause. "As some of you who are familiar with the band know, a lot of my writing comes from the stupid things I've done. And I'll be the first to admit that I've dug my own grave a few times." There are a few approving screams from the audience. "But sometimes something wonderful comes into your life that forces you to man up. So this song is for that radiant person."

I refuse to even look at Emme. I already know she's staring at the floor.

My hands are shaking as I smooth out the piece of paper with the words on it and set it on the floor. It's a page from the notebook Emme gave me at Christmas.

I start to pick a melody from the guitar and then sing:

There are so many words bottled up inside
They scream out to be released
You've cast a spell over me
Been blinded for long, but can now see

You're the only thing that matters in my life
All that I've done is for you
The biggest piece, the biggest part
The one person who controls my heart

If I could kiss away your pain, I would
If I could hold you every night, I would
If I could erase every mistake, every other face
I wouldn't change a thing
Because all those things led me to this place
And to you

Because I . . . I could never break your heart
I wouldn't know where to start
All I know to be true
Is the only breaking will be done by you

If I could make you smile all day, I would
If I could be the person you want, I would
If I could erase every mistake, every other face

I wouldn't change a thing
Because all those things led me to this place
And to you

Because I . . . I could never break your heart
I wouldn't know where to start
All I know to be true
Is the only breaking will be done by you

The last note hangs in the air. I grab the lyrics from the floor and head off the stage. I hear the crowd reacting, but I don't care. It wasn't for them. It never has been.

I turn for the first time to see her reaction. Her eyes are wide, her lips are pursed, her face pale. She looks down at the ground as I approach. Ben grabs Jack and they walk away.

"Emme." I see her shiver slightly.

She starts shaking her head. She's saying something, but I can't hear her over the crowd.

I lean in so I'm close to her. "I'm sorry," she says.

My entire body aches at her apology. "Because you don't have feelings for me?"

She looks up at me and I can tell she's mad. "I do have feelings for you, Ethan. That's the problem. We're best friends, you're the closest person in the world to me. Why can't we just keep things the way they are now?"

"Because I love you."

"And I love you, too."

I've wanted to hear those words from her for so long. Although I know her love and my love are two very different things. "But just not in that way, right?"

She doesn't respond. I feel a madness creep over me. I need to get out of here, away from Emme.

I hear a voice call out after me. But it's not Emme's voice, so I don't care.

A hand wraps itself tightly around my arm. "Ethan, are you okay?"

It's Ben. I yank my arm free.

"I can't do this anymore."

I turn my back and walk away from Emme, from the band, from my life.

EMME

always knew that senior year would be full of challenges — the showcase, the school auditions, leaving CPA behind.

But never did I imagine that the hardest part of senior year would be losing two people who mean so much to me.

What's odd is that I didn't even really feel the loss of Sophie. I found that I had a lot more time to focus on my music and the band.

But Ethan . . . watching him slip away has been harder than I could've ever imagined.

Sure, he's still in class, but he keeps to himself. He hardly looks at me anymore. He won't commit to any more shows. It's like he's shut himself off from us.

And it's all my fault.

When he confessed his feelings for me, I was so torn. Part of me wanted to kiss him and not hesitate to jump into a relationship with him. But another part of me was scared. And that part won.

Then I froze after he sang that song.

I was scared of losing Ethan. But I lost him anyway.

And every time I see him, I'm reminded of what a mistake I've made.

It's been two weeks since our concert. It has been the emptiest two weeks of my life. I've tried to talk to him, but it doesn't work.

I head to my locker after class. While packing my bag, I open my phone and check my e-mail. I have one from Carter telling me he's passed the GED. I'm about to e-mail him back when another message comes in. A chill rushes through me as I see the one e-mail I've been waiting for my entire life.

"Hey, Red!" Jack comes up to me. "I got this —"

"Have you seen Ethan?" I blurt out.

Jack stops and points toward the exit. "He was walking out the —"

I sprint toward the door and run down the street to try to catch Ethan. I weave through the mass of students heading home and the tourists going to Lincoln Center. I've walked to Ethan's house with him so many times that I have his route memorized. I turn the corner and spot his red and gray back-pack in the distance. I ignore the sharp pain in my side and continue to run.

I try calling out his name, but he has his earphones in and can't hear me. I'm less than a block away. I concentrate on him and nearly run over a group of tourists trying to take a picture.

"ETHAN!" I scream, although I know he can't hear me.

I'm only a few feet away from him and I reach my hand out to tap him. He stops dead in his tracks and I run right into him.

Before I know what hits me, I find myself lying on the sidewalk. Ethan's eyes are wide as he takes out his headphones. "Are you okay?"

He reaches down and helps me up.

"What's goin' on over here?" A police offer approaches us. "Did you not see the traffic light?"

I brush the dirt off my pants. "Sorry, officer. I was trying to catch up to my friend." I'm trying to catch my breath; all the cold air is burning my lungs.

"You could've gotten hit by a car." He shakes his head and goes back to directing traffic.

The light changes, and Ethan and I cross the street.

He finally speaks. "What was that all about?"

"Sorry, I was trying to catch up to you. I didn't see that you were at a crosswalk."

"No, I mean, why are you here?"

I stop walking. "Ethan, I got into Juilliard."

His face lights up. "Emme, congratulations!" It's the first smile I've seen from him in weeks. He gives me one of his Ethan hugs. I thought I missed him, but being here with him, in his arms, makes the reality of what I lost much more traumatic.

"But that's not what I wanted to talk to you about. I mean, it is. But . . ." I try to compose myself. I didn't really have a plan but to find him. "When I saw the e-mail, you were the first person I thought of. It's like nothing happens to me unless you know about it. And it's like these last two weeks didn't exist because you weren't a part of them. My biggest fear this entire time was losing you, but all I was doing was pushing you away. I don't want you to be away. I want you to be here. I need you, and not because of the band or because you help me, but because I love you. And as much as I was trying to pretend that it was just in a friendly way, it wasn't.

"You being with Kelsey made me not ever have to come to terms with my feelings for you. And the reason I got so mad at you for cheating was because I always felt like you were cheating on me as well. And when you two finally broke up, it frightened me. Because then *I* was going to have to figure out how I really felt. When I think back to the alumni night, the memory that sticks in my head isn't being onstage, it is afterward when you kissed me. And then when you apologized I thought you saw me like those girls who throw themselves at you during our shows. But *I* never regretted that kiss. The only thing I regret is that I didn't have the courage to take a chance on us."

Ethan entwines his hand in mine. "Let's walk."

"Oh." I'm surprised and a little disappointed that's all he has to say to me.

"We need to stop having these conversations in front of people." He gestures toward the group of people drinking coffee outside. "Plus, it would be nice to not have an audience when I kiss you again."

The shortness of breath I have is no longer from running.

"So I'm going to need you to excuse me because it is going to be very hard for me to contain myself for the next three blocks."

Ethan doesn't say anything, but picks up his pace as we walk into his apartment building. We stand only inches apart in the elevator and I find myself utterly aware of his presence.

He stays silent until we get to his room. He turns around and studies me. I've seen that look one other time from him and it was before he kissed me.

"Wait!" It takes me a second to realize that came from me. "I'm sorry, I just I need you to know something. . . ."

He sits down on his bed. "I need to tell you something first."

A numbness falls over me. Did I just ruin the moment? Last time he said that to me, he made a wonderful confession. I'm not so sure this time.

"I didn't get into Juilliard."

I collapse on his bed. "What?"

"It's okay, really it is." He rubs my back. Why is *he* comforting *me*?

"When did you find out?"

"Yesterday. I didn't want to say anything until you knew about your application. I don't want this to change how you feel. It's unbelievably incredible, Emme. You should be really proud of yourself."

Ethan didn't get in, but I did? Out of all the confusing things to have happened this year, this is the one thing that makes the least sense.

"I'm going to the Manhattan School of Music."

"What about Berklee?"

"I don't want to leave New York. There are too many things that are changing as is. I don't want to move to another city on top of it all. And, to be honest, you getting into Juilliard confirms I made the right decision. My parents wrote out the deposit check last night." He looks at me hopefully.

"Oh." I move closer to him.

Ethan moves his hand so it's around my waist and he rests his chin on my shoulder.

"We did it." My quivering voice betrays the calm façade I'm trying to maintain being so close to him.

"Yes, we did. I'm so proud of you, Emme. I truly am."

I rest my head against his and we sit there quietly for a few minutes. I try to comprehend everything that has changed in the last hour or so. I know my fate: I'm going to Juilliard. And Ethan will be in Manhattan.

"So what did you want to tell me?" he finally asks. "Please don't say you're taking back what you said to me outside. Because those words will never leave my mind."

I pull away so I can look into his eyes. "No, I don't take those back. I'm really sorry about the past few weeks. I was just overwhelmed."

"There was a lot going on."

He's always been understanding, but I know I'm not being clear. Oddly enough, my stress had nothing to do with school coming to an end.

"No, I've been overwhelmed by *you*. You overwhelm me . . . in the best possible sense. You once told me that you wish I could see myself through your eyes, but I can. Because I've always seen how you look at me. I didn't know it was possible to be loved in the way you love me. I've always kind of thought that kind of love was the stuff of movies and cheesy ballads. I didn't think it existed and I'll admit, it frightened me. What if I couldn't live up to your image of me? What if once you got me, I wouldn't be enough? But I'm not fighting it. I want to be with you."

Ethan smiles and pulls me closer. "So does this mean I get to take you on a proper date?"

I giggle nervously. We know each other so well and have gone out to eat so many times, I wonder how differently things will feel on an "official" date?

"Hmm, I guess you can take me to dinner to celebrate."

"That I can do."

I lean in. "And maybe write a song about how you saw your way to forgive a silly girl."

"That I won't do."

I don't even have time to be disappointed by his reaction. He cups his hand around my face. "Because you've done nothing wrong. And you're here now. That's all that matters."

We kiss. And at no point does either of us pull away or apologize.

Because we don't have anything to be sorry for.

Graduation

SOPHIE

J can't wait for this ridiculous ceremony to get over
with so I can move on with my life.

After Emme decided to shove a knife in my back, I realized that CPA doesn't *deserve* to showcase my talent. So I waited
out the last few months of school. I wasn't going to waste my
time auditioning for parts that nobody wants me to have. I'll
never understand what these administrators have against me.
Probably they know that I have more talent in my pinky than
the entire faculty combined.

They'll be begging me to come back and speak to future
classes. I'll be on that screen. They'll be bragging about me. I
can't wait to turn them down.

Starting tomorrow, I can do what I want. I won't have anybody holding me back. No teachers, no Sarah Moffitt, no Emme.

I'll have my CPA diploma. And let me just say that my education here has certainly prepared me for the real world.

If you can survive having your alleged best friend betray you, what's the worst thing a casting director can do?

In one hour, I'll be free.

I'll have a new Plan that doesn't revolve around anybody but me.

Next step — Sophie Jenkins, superstar.

Check.

CARTER

While I'm sitting only a dozen or so rows behind the graduating class, I feel like I'm a world away from the student I was when I started here.

I've got a long way to go, but I'm working on painting and getting my portfolio ready for my own auditions for art school next year.

My last episode of the soap aired two weeks ago. I enjoyed the media attention this time around, because I knew I was ending a chapter of my life and beginning a new one.

I'm not sure where any of this will lead me, but for the first time, I'm taking charge of my life. I'm not acting. I'm being me.

That's all I ever wanted.

ETHAN

'm well aware that I have a goofy grin on my face while an Oscar-winning alumna gives our commencement address. It has nothing to do with whatever it is she's saying.

I've got a lot to smile for. I'm staying in New York to study music, I'm with the one person I've longed to be with, and, above all, there's silence.

For the first time in my life, those screaming voices in my head have disappeared.

The only thoughts that circle my mind are happy and practically serene.

And, of course, the dominant thought that controls my mind is love.

The love of Emme, the love of my family, the love of my friends, and the love that I finally have for myself.

I can't wait to see what I can do, now that I'm no longer standing in my own way.

EMME

The four of us wait in the wings. Ethan playfully flicks at the tassel on my cap.

Ben puts his arm around us. "You know, it was hard enough trying to get a song featured when we had to compete against you two separately, but when you decide to write a song *together*, what hope does any of us have? Although I don't mind being the Harrison to your Lennon/McCartney."

"Wait, are you calling *me* Ringo?" Jack opens his mouth in mock horror. "Well, kids, it's our last official show as CPA students. I know this isn't lunch, but I figure . . ."

Jack holds up his hand as the three of us protest. We thought the days of hearing about our demise were over.

He grabs us and we get into a huddle. "The rise of Teenage Kicks at CPA was a magical experience. After graduation the four talented musicians have to go their separate ways to college: dashing charismatic leader Jack to sunny California, where he will become a famous movie composer; the quiet yet strong Ben to Oberlin to be a producer; and then the power couple Emme Connelly and Ethan Quinn staying in Manhattan, who will no doubt become a songwriting duo to be reckoned with. And while the foursome will be apart, they will forever have a piece of each other's hearts."

I feel tears sting behind my eyes. I never expected Jack to be so sentimental, especially before we have to perform.

"I love you guys," he says. We all hug. Ethan grabs me and gives me a kiss.

"Get a room," Jack teases.

We hear our names called out to perform the song Ethan and I wrote together.

The four of us step onto the stage and into the spotlight.

Where we belong.

A C K N O W L E D G M E N T S

It feels extremely appropriate to do a curtain call for all of the
people who are responsible for making this book, and Author
Elizabeth, a reality.

Everybody at Scholastic for working behind the scenes on
my books. A standing ovation for Erin Black, Elizabeth Parisi,
Sheila Marie Everett, Tracy van Straaten, Bess Braswell, Emily
Sharpe, Leslie Garych, Ruth Mirsky, Joy Simpkins, and all of the
sales reps. I'm ready for a few more encores if you are!

Bravo to my friends who've helped me along the way. Jennifer
Leonard for once again coming to the rescue with your reader
comments. The lovely David Shannon for answering my art ques-
tions. Kirk Benshoff for making my website sparkle and shine.
T. S. Ferguson for brainstorming so, so many possible titles.
Natalie Thrasher for helping me stay semi-sane (no easy feat!).

It was my love of music and playing it throughout my life
that led me to write this book. I'd like to thank my mom for pay-
ing for all those music lessons. My siblings (Eileen, Meg, and
WJ) who didn't make fun of me *too* much while I practiced. And,
of course, my father, who had to put up with all of us. I'd also
like to give a big shout-out to all of my music teachers through
the years, especially Carol Larrabee, Michael Tentis (aka "T"),

and the guys at the Guitar Bar in Hoboken (I still like to think I earned that Student of the Week award, and it wasn't because I wore you down).

I'm inspired every day by music. So many of my favorite artists influenced this book, especially my magical friend Marketa Irglova for lifting the backstage curtain so I could see what it's *really* like to be in a band, and the superb Gary Lightbody for his beautiful lyrics that helped me whenever I needed some motivation.

I've been fortunate to have so many author friends in my life, first as a publicist and now as an author. It means the world to me to have the support of wonderful and talented friends who understand that having voices in your head can be a good thing.

Finally, a bouquet of roses to all of the booksellers, librarians, and bloggers who have been so enthusiastic about my books. I'm truly honored and humbled by your support and hope we've got a long road ahead of us.